The Stuff

Nell had almost gotten up her courage to ask Sir Hugh about his family when the carriage drew up in front of the house in Queen Square. She waited while he helped Aunt Longstreet down from the cab. When he subsequently took Nell's hand, she was forced to grasp his firmly as she forced her bustled gown through the cab's doorway.

In her eagerness to find herself firmly on the ground, she slid slightly on the step, and Sir Hugh's other hand came instantly to her waist to support her. His aid lasted only a moment, as she was soon safely on the pavement. Oh, it was the smallest of actions, but Nell chose to tuck it, along with the sensation it aroused in her, away in her mind. It was the sort of detail one needed to embellish a daydream, and she might have great need of daydreams when she returned with her aunt to Longstreet Manor. . . .

For Kay Turner, without whose enthusiastic encouragement and generous assistance this project could not have been completed.
Many, many thanks!

Chapter One

Nell was beginning to think it had not been a good idea to come to Bath. In fact, she was pretty sure it was an alarmingly bad idea. When she had been alone with Aunt Longstreet in the manor house in Westmorland, her aunt had seemed eccentric but harmless. There, one could discount the very odd things she was given to saying to the vicar and the neighbors as merely the whim of a rich woman whose acquaintances understood her queer starts.

In Bath, the case was otherwise.

Nell had accompanied her aunt to Bath for the waters, though heaven knew her aunt, at sixty, had the energy of a thirty-year-old. A mere month ago Aunt Longstreet had frowned over a letter she'd received, then said abruptly, "Gretchen Dorsey insists that Bath is the place to go for any indisposition. Taking the waters has decidedly beneficial effects on any manner of problem—especially gout, she says. I want you to arrange it, Helen."

Well, there was no choice, really. What Aunt Longstreet wanted, Nell was perforce required to do. Not that her aunt had ever taken such a notion into her head before. Nell had lived with her at Longstreet Manor for ten years now, and although her aunt did have a touch of gout from time to time, prior to this start she hadn't shown the least inclination to relocate so far as the nearest spa. She seldom ventured into the village, which was half a mile distant, and only attended church in order to discompose the vicar, so far as Nell could see.

But Bath, once decided upon, had become an obsession with her aunt. She sent away for guidebooks, and solicited advice from her more well-traveled neighbors on where to let a house, and how much one should expect to pay. She seemed to have taken it into her head, even before this advice was solicited, that they should be located in or near Queen Square. Nell had never been to Bath, but she could see on the map her aunt spread out on the marble top of the rosewood table that Queen Square was a promising location, and she made no objection to being there.

Perhaps from the circumstance of her never having been anywhere at all, save in the North Country, Nell had thought it would be quite a delightful change of pace. Little had she imagined . . .

She watched her aunt now, as the older lady thumped her way around the circulating library on Milsom Street. Nell had been especially eager to visit this popular spot, understanding that there were untold quantities of novels to be found here, in addition to such enlightening reading as sermons and histories. Aunt Longstreet seemed to have some other object to her visit, however, than to find a suitable volume to carry home to their rented house.

With her cane acting as both support and weapon, the persistent lady pushed herself through a small circle of conversing women, who looked at first surprised and then alarmed. "Make way, make way," Aunt Longstreet muttered. "Flock of chattering birds. Can't you see you're in the way?"

The women did indeed move aside, since Rosemarie Longstreet had her cane raised like a sword, jabbing it in front of her. Nell knew it was of no use to expostulate with the woman, so she did nothing more than flash quick smiles at the dispersing ladies to indicate her sympathy and inability to curb her aunt's reckless passage.

"If they wish to chatter, why don't they do so out on the pavement?" Aunt Longstreet demanded. She raised her cane to drum it loudly on the desk in the center of the room. "Young man! Attend me!"

Though the poor fellow was dealing with another patron, he had the good sense to take in the situation at a glance and instantly excused himself. "Yes, ma'am? How may I be of assistance?" he asked as he cautiously approached.

"You may find me a Peerage," she informed him haughtily.

"If perhaps you would indicate where I might find it," Nell interposed, "I'm sure I would be happy to search it out."

The young man turned to her with a slight hesitation. He was a mildly attractive man, tall and thin with a serious mien. "They're along the west wall, miss. Second shelf from the top. We don't circulate them, though. You'll have to study them here."

"Not circulate them!" her aunt exploded. "Never heard of such a thing! And you call yourselves a circulating library!"

"They're a reference tool," the young man informed her stoutly. "Most of our patrons have no need to drag one of those weighty old tomes home with them."

"Well, I don't intend to waste my time in this murky room, ruining my eyes while I look up the information I'm seeking," she informed him. "I had every intention of taking the volumes off with me."

"I'm afraid that won't be possible." Every eye in the room was now on the young man and his challenger. "However," he continued, adjusting his eyeglasses rather higher on his nose, "if you were interested in purchasing last year's set, I would be at liberty to sell it to you for a very modest sum."

"Last year's set? Why would I want last year's set?" Aunt Longstreet demanded.

"The information changes very little," he assured her, looking around at his audience in hopes of receiving some assistance. "You know, there are a few births, a few deaths, that sort of thing. Most of the information remains the same."

"Most of it! As though that would be good enough for me. I want the most current, accurate information possible."

"Aunt Longstreet," Nell said quietly, taking her aunt's arm, "I would be pleased to do any research you had in mind and bring the information home to you. You needn't strain your eyes or purchase an outdated set. Just inform me of your needs, and I shall manage the whole."

Miss Longstreet narrowed her eyes at her niece and said firmly, "That won't do, my girl. It's got naught to do with you. If this facility is unable to accommodate my needs, we shall find one that can."

The young man was unwise enough to say, "But we're the only circulating library in Bath, ma'am."

"Infamous!" she pronounced. "I see how it is! You have stomped upon the competition and now refuse to offer what your patrons demand. Oh, that is always the way. Don't think that I shall darken your doors again!"

Nell distinctly heard someone say, "Thank heaven," but she believed it was one of the women and not the young man, whose face had become suffused with color. "I'm very sorry for it, ma'am," he said, as though to atone for the unfortunate comment.

"Perhaps," said an entirely different male voice, "I might be of assistance to you, Miss Longstreet."

The two women turned to find a man dressed in the first style of elegance approaching them from the doorway. He bowed gracefully and tucked his hat under his arm. "Hugh Nowlin, at your service."

Rosemarie Longstreet glared at the young man and muttered only one word, "Dandy!"

He laughed at her epithet, but did glance down at his Hessian boots. "Do you think so? Perhaps the tassels are a bit *de trop*, what? I shall have them removed."

"Not on my account," she snapped. "You may dress entirely as you wish, Hugh Nowlin."

"Thank you, ma'am. And this would be your niece, Helen Armstrong, I believe. How do you do, ma'am?"

Nell curtsied but regarded him with curiosity, though his name was familiar enough. She believed that some stigma was attached to it—at least in her aunt's eyes. He was of medium height, with brown hair and blue eyes, eyes that were deeply amused at the moment. The sparkle this gave his expression was not at all unattractive. "Mr. Nowlin," she acknowledged.

"Sir Hugh," her aunt corrected, though in no pleasant tone of voice. "My godson."

"And a great favorite with her, as you see," the gentleman offered. "Come, Miss Longstreet, let me escort you down the street to Mollands at number 2. Nothing is so likely to sweeten your disposition as one of their pastries."

He placed her hand on his right arm and indicated that Nell should take his other. Hesitating, she placed her fingers on his jacket sleeve, barely touching him, but glad for the opportunity to leave the premises under something less of a cloud. Aunt Longstreet sniffed and thumped her cane on the floor before deciding that she was willing to allow her godson to lead her away. Nell had the liveliest fear that her aunt would make one more disagreeable remark about the library before exiting, so she was relieved when their escort inclined his head toward her aunt and said, "I do mean to assist you, you know. I have a set of the latest Peerage at my apartments in the Crescent."

"And why would you have the Peerage?" she demanded. "The Baronetage would be more suitable."

"Oh, I have aspirations," he teased, his eyes merry. "You have no idea what aspirations I have."

"Nodcock."

Since her aunt's disparagements only seemed to amuse the young man, Nell relaxed a little and allowed her hand to rest more firmly on his arm. It was a pleasant May day outside, with a light breeze to sway her sprigged muslin gown and toy with her black ringlets. Traversing the busy shopping street on the arm of a respectable escort was no disagreeable sensation, either. In fact, she thought, catching the warmth of attentive interest in his expression as he glanced down at her, the sensation was downright agreeable.

Reality all too soon intruded. Her aunt, on the doorstep of the pastry cook shop, refused to budge another step. "I don't wish to have a sweet," she protested. "It is only three hours since I broke my fast."

Sir Hugh, undaunted by his stubborn godmother, held open the door. "Indeed, ma'am, but I am convinced that Miss Armstrong is in need of refreshment. Nothing is so restorative as a cup of tea and a Bath bun, don't you agree, Miss Armstrong?"

Nell blinked in astonishment at this appeal to herself. What had she to say to anything? But the young man continued to regard her, his brows raised, and she said, "I should be very grateful for a cup of tea, sir."

"Oh, very well," Aunt Longstreet agreed with poor grace. "Don't know what's the matter with you young folks—forever fading away for lack of a little starch in your spines."

"We can't all have as much starch as you," Sir Hugh murmured as his godmother proceeded into the shop. He gave Nell a quick, commiserating grin as she passed by him. Nell thought perhaps she shouldn't allow herself to side with this stranger against her aunt and kept her countenance noncommittal.

Mollands was not a destination her aunt had previously

approved, so Nell looked about her with interest. The wrought-iron tables with their marble tops were accompanied by curlicued wrought-iron chairs that did not look very comfortable. Yet the place was full of fashionable people and was filled with the most delightful aromas of baking pastries. Nell's mouth watered at the thought of a tasty treat, and she moved carefully to the counter where a variety of baked goods was displayed. Bath buns were the very least of these items, looking entirely uninteresting when compared to the macaroons, the ratafia cakes, and the almond cake.

"I'm partial to the plum cake myself," Sir Hugh said from beside her, "but my sister has always favored the gingerbread."

Nell could see that the thick gingerbread squares were more expensive than the plum cake, but both seemed most unreasonable to her. In the village they wouldn't have cost half as much. Her gaze moved quickly from one item to the next and alighted at length on the Scotch shortbread for only a penny a piece. "I believe I would like the shortbread," she said.

Sir Hugh regarded her searchingly for a moment and said, "Very well. Your aunt insists that she wants nothing but tea. Do you think we could tempt her with a Savoy cake?"

"Well," Nell said frankly, "she would very much enjoy it, but if she has set her mind to having nothing but tea, you may be sure that she would not eat a Savoy cake, even if it appeared in front of her."

"Yes, as I feared," he said gravely.

They retreated to a table where Aunt Longstreet was already seated, and Sir Hugh held Nell's chair for her. He claimed the attention of the serving maid, but consulted with the girl in so moderate a voice that Nell was unable to overhear what he ordered. This was partially because her aunt had taken exception to the paint scheme of the room and was expounding on its lack of appropriateness.

"Gold and purple," she muttered. "As though they were pastry cook to the king. What, may I ask, would be amiss with a coat of whitewash and a few bright paintings on the walls? That's the problem with Bath. Everything is overdone. You cannot go anywhere that you see any simplicity. Crescents and Circuses and Squares until you are quite disgusted with such a display."

"Oh, I think Bath is beautiful," Nell sighed. "So elegant. All the buildings of that lovely stone. The architecture so consistent. Why, there's scarcely a building here over a hundred years old."

"Precisely," said her aunt.

Sir Hugh smiled. "Not at all like Longstreet Manor, eh? That old mausoleum must have wings dating from the fourteen hundreds. With all their inconveniences as well, I daresay."

"Tradition, heritage, ancestry," Aunt Longstreet informed him, as she often did Nell. "Nothing could be more important, my boy. All this trumpery modern finery is not to be compared with the solidity of the past."

"All this modern trumpery," Sir Hugh said dolefully, "will become the heritage of the next generations, ma'am. No way to stop the march of progress."

"Progress, ha! Degradation, more like." Aunt Longstreet observed the items that the serving girl placed upon the table and frowned. "I want nothing but tea," she protested. "As I told you."

"Indeed, ma'am. But my own appetite is healthy, and I believe your companion shares my appreciation of fine bakery goods."

Nell eyed the collection of items with something like awe. He had ordered the plum cake, and the gingerbread, and the Scotch shortbread, and a Savoy cake, as well as their tea. She was not quite certain if she was to be allotted more than one choice of these delectables, and she glanced inquiringly at her host.

"Please help yourself," the baronet urged. "Between us we should be able to polish off the whole, don't you think?"

"I shouldn't be at all surprised," she said, a smile blooming on her face at his obvious determination to provide her with what he must know was an unaccustomed treat. Well, so it was! She helped herself to the gingerbread and took a daintily greedy bite. The thick square was still warm, and the taste of treacle delighted her tongue. "Oh, Aunt Longstreet, it's better than Cook's!" she exclaimed.

"I doubt that very much," her aunt said crossly.

"Well, just as good," Nell temporized. "And Cook's never comes to the table warm."

"No wonder," Sir Hugh interjected. "The kitchens at Longstreet Manor must be miles away from the dining parlor."

"Oh, you've been there, have you?" Nell asked innocently as she forked another bite.

"Of course he has!" Aunt Longstreet snapped. "He's my godson."

"But I've been with you ten years, Aunt, and he hasn't come while I've been there."

"Very true," the young man acknowledged, that wicked twinkle back in his eyes as his gaze held Nell's. She felt an odd little flutter in her breast. "I fear I have displeased my godmother, and the open invitation I used to enjoy has been withdrawn. But in the past I spent many happy days at the Manor."

"Hogwash," his godmother said. "You always found it sadly flat there. No chance for the racketing about you delighted in elsewhere."

He nodded. "And I was terrified to bring my cattle there, you know, Miss Armstrong. Shabbiest stables I've ever seen, and if the groom is under fifty I should be vastly surprised."

"He is a trifle old," Nell agreed, "but he's been there forever and knows just what my aunt wishes. Of course, with only the one helper, it's no use Aunt Longstreet attempting to stable a visitor's horses. But then," she said matter-of-factly, "we seldom have visitors."

"Never, I should have thought," he murmured.

"Mind your tongue, young man," Aunt Longstreet said. "I'll have that Savoy cake after all, since Helen doesn't need anything else after that enormous chunk of gingerbread."

Nell hid her disappointment with a perfunctory smile. When Sir Hugh placed the shortbread in front of her, she shook her head. "No, no, that's for you," she insisted.

"Not at all! It's what you asked for to begin with," he said, leaving it where he'd placed it. "Personally I'd prefer another plum cake, and I shall summon one up."

"Pure indulgence," grunted Aunt Longstreet, who was in the process of demolishing the splendid little Savoy cake in three bites.

"Yes, but that's precisely what you can expect of the youth of today," Sir Hugh confided to Nell. "I'm sure your Aunt Longstreet has mentioned that."

The corners of Nell's mouth twitched, but she returned no answer.

"I've had better Savoy cake," Aunt Longstreet announced as she regarded her empty plate with disfavor.

"Naturally," her godson said.

"And better tea. A little on the weak side, for my taste," she said mildly, disposing herself comfortably in her chair. "But we'll come again, Helen, for I see that this establishment is patronized by a very good class of people. Better than the Pump Room, I daresay."

"You've been to the Pump Room already?" Sir Hugh

asked, looking surprised. "I thought perhaps you'd just arrived in Bath."

"We've been here a week," Nell explained when her aunt seemed to ignore his remark. "Aunt Longstreet has taken a house in Queen Square."

"Queen Square! Lovely, I'm sure, but the oldest of the squares in Bath, if I'm not mistaken."

"Which is precisely why we're there," Aunt Longstreet informed him. "Built in 1734 and therefore has some history. No doubt it seems old-fashioned to you."

"No, no, merely quiet and without some of the conveniences of the more recent squares and the Crescent. If you're headed in that direction, I should be pleased to escort you home."

Aunt Longstreet hesitated, and Nell did nothing to indicate her preference in the matter. Her aunt was so contrary that if Nell were to say, "Oh, that would be kind of you," her aunt would probably dismiss the young man on the instant! But Aunt Longstreet must have had a reason to accommodate the fellow, for she said at length, "Very well. We were through with our errands for the morning."

The distance between Milsom Street and Queen Square was no more than a few blocks. Aunt Longstreet, despite the cane, was not one to dawdle, so they covered the whole of it in less than ten minutes. Nell would have enjoyed strolling along looking into the shopwindows and thus extending for a few more moments what had proved to be an exceptionally pleasant excursion, but her aunt scorned such a waste of time. Sir Hugh kept up a steady stream of inconsequential chatter about the town and its pleasures.

"I trust you've signed the master of ceremony's book," he said as they came within sight of number 10.

"No, why should we?" Aunt Longstreet demanded. "We're not here for the dancing."

"You don't intend to visit the Lower Rooms?"

"Certainly not. Too expensive, too crowded, too hot. I know what these rooms are, and I cannot think I would find any pleasure in them."

Sir Hugh frowned. "Perhaps you would not, Miss Longstreet, but your companion most assuredly would. Miss Armstrong is young and needs to meet others of her age. You cannot bring her from the wilds of Westmorland to such a lively place as Bath and expect her to do no more than dance attendance upon you."

Nell flushed at such a harsh rendering of the situation. Though it was more or less true, she would never, ever have said anything of the sort. She was wholly dependent upon Aunt Longstreet, and she had known from the time the expedition was planned that her aunt could no more be expected to put herself out to chaperone her niece to the assemblies in Bath than she could be expected to fly. At the time the arrangements were made, however, Nell had believed that it would be quite enough for her to see all the glories of the town. She had never suspected how much she would long to partake of the glamorous entertainments.

Aunt Longstreet was unaccustomed to criticism of her actions. She scowled at Sir Hugh and informed him that it was no business of his what she did. "Helen has neither the inclination nor the wardrobe to be gallivanting off to dances in strange towns with strange men for partners. She is of a serious, not a frivolous, disposition."

Sir Hugh turned to Nell, but she lowered her gaze before his intense scrutiny, and said nothing. "I see," he murmured at length. "Well, I wish you a pleasant stay in Bath, Miss Longstreet. Please do not hesitate to call upon me if I may be of any service to you."

"I'm sure we shall not be in need of any services which you could provide," Aunt Longstreet sniffed as she thumped her cane against the door of their rented house.

"Your servant, Miss Armstrong," he said, bowing politely.

After such a pointed rebuff, Nell doubted they would see the man ever again. She felt an unaccountable pang, whether from continuing embarrassment or regret, she wasn't sure. "Thank you for the lovely pastries, Sir Hugh, and for seeing us home."

"My pleasure."

He turned then, as though easily dismissing them from his mind, and strolled off down the street.

Chapter Two

But Sir Hugh was far from dismissing the two ladies from his mind. He had been acquainted with Miss Longstreet from the moment of his birth, and he had a good knowledge of her character. Though she had doted on him as child and young lad, she had pretty much dismissed him when he reached an age to join the adult world. Sir Hugh suspected that Miss Longstreet wasn't overfond of men in general.

He did remember with pleasure the summers he had visited at Longstreet Manor as a child. Of course, Miss Longstreet's parents had still been alive then, and with their complicity he had been indulged most shamefully. They kept a pony for him when he was very young, and a horse as he grew older. Perhaps that was the lure which drew him to Longstreet Manor—that horse he had been so fond of.

His own parents were kindly but not so indulgent as the elder Longstreets and their spinster daughter. Every treat was provided for his entertainment and enjoyment—games of cricket with the neighboring boys, visits to the closest market town to find him a special pair of riding gloves, an extensive library put at his disposal. They were halcyon days, remembered with great fondness. His sister Emily had greatly envied him those visits, as she was not included in the annual invitation.

Sir Hugh had not intended to head for his apartments in

the Crescent, but he found himself turning from Gay Street into the Circus, and, shrugging, continued around the circle to Brook Street. Even now he could have changed his mind, as his friend Hopkins had rooms along that very block, but Sir Hugh found himself unwilling to disrupt his train of thought. There was something most unusual about finding his godmother in Bath, and he had every intention of figuring out what had brought her there.

No one was going to hoax him into believing that she was there for the waters. He was well aware that Miss Longstreet suffered occasionally from the gout, but he believed he knew her well enough to realize that she would not come such a distance away from her home on the off chance that the mineral waters would dissipate her goutish pains. She was far too complacent about her own physical condition to make any such effort. It was his impression that Miss Longstreet prided herself on her ability to withstand any amount of discomfort. Attempting to alleviate it by such an exercise as taking the waters in a town so far from Longstreet Manor simply didn't ring true.

And there was the niece—Miss Armstrong. He had known his godmother had taken in an impoverished relative, but he had believed the woman to be much more advanced in years than the young lady he'd met in Milsom Street. He had, in fact, supposed her to be much closer in age to her benefactor. Sir Hugh was not at all sure he liked the idea of Miss Armstrong, who could be no more than twenty-four or twenty-five, ingratiating herself with *his* godmother.

An odd sort of girl she was, too. Not willing to speak up for herself, and yet not entirely cowed by Miss Longstreet, he thought. Sir Hugh suspected that there was more to the young woman than appeared beneath her air of quiet composure. No doubt Miss Armstrong had learned to "manage" her patron, neither opposing nor distressing the cantankerous lady, but not giving Miss Longstreet a dislike of her by proving mealymouthed, either. Rosemarie Longstreet would not tolerate a weakling around her.

Yes, Sir Hugh suspected Miss Armstrong had used her many years with that good lady to advantage; she had determined to a nicety just how far she dared go with his godmother and yet retain that woman's esteem. And, loath though he was to admit it, he felt a certain anxiety.

Sir Hugh had long believed that he was to inherit his godmother's estate. That had been the intention when his own parents chose Miss Longstreet as his godmother. His mother and Miss Longstreet had become fast friends during their come-outs in London lo these many years ago. And apparently by the time Hugh was born, there was no question but that Miss Longstreet had become an old maid and that she would inherit Longstreet Manor. Since that delightful estate must devolve somewhere, why not to Sir Hugh? Now it had come as something of a shock to realize how much he'd come to count on that expectation.

"Oh, Hugh, I had thought to catch you at the library," a lilting voice informed him before he had raised his frowning gaze from the pavement to notice that his sister was approaching.

"Had you, by Jove? And why had you reason to believe you would find me there, Emily?"

"Because you told Hammer that is where you were headed." She cocked her head at him, her blue eyes, so like his own, challenging. "I trust you found something enlightening there, for I know you would scorn to waste your time reading a novel."

"Actually, I found my godmother there, berating the librarian because she could not carry off the current Peerage."

"Miss Longstreet is here, in Bath?"

"You may well be shocked, my dear sister. Who would have thought it, eh? But indeed it was she, accompanied by a Miss Armstrong, the woman who has lived with her these past ten years."

Emily's gaze sharpened. "A woman not to your taste, Hugh?"

"As to that, she's a trifle tall for my liking, but it was her age that surprised me. She cannot be more than five and twenty."

Her brows rose. "So young? And how does she cope with Miss Longstreet's vile temper?"

"That's what I've just been musing on, my dear." He glanced at the footman, who was following to accompany his mistress on her errands. "Send Williams home, and I'll walk you to the library if you wish."

"Very well." When the footman had been dismissed, Emily Holmsly linked arms with her brother, peering curiously up at him. "Something you didn't want Williams to hear, Hugh?"

He shrugged. "I have less tolerance for being the subject of servants' gossip than you do, Emily dearest."

A flush rose to her cheeks. "Really, Hugh, that is unjust. I have never given my servants the least reason to gossip about me, I assure you."

"Have you not? I wonder, then, that one should hear your name bandied about so freely in the Pump Room. Yesterday, there was something about a cicisbeo being slapped by you, I believe."

"Well, my word! That is the outside of enough!" she exclaimed, indignant. "My name is muddied because Frederickson goes beyond the line of what is pleasing. Really, Hugh, you should rather have a word with that ramshackle young man. He tried to kiss me! Word of honor, I did nothing to encourage him."

"Nothing but be the most adorable woman in town, with a habit of attracting men of his caliber like filings to a magnet." He waved aside her protest. "No, no, don't tell me it is not your fault. I quite understand that you are unable to protect yourself from such hangers-on. I believe Holmsly would do well to take a little better care of you."

To his vast surprise, tears sprang to her eyes and she dug awkwardly in her reticule for a handkerchief. She turned aside from him, dabbing at her eyes, and eventually discreetly blew her nose on the flimsy piece of fabric. "Holmsly," she managed to say, "is from town—again."

"Devil take the man! I thought he had brought you here to spend a little time in your company after your confinement. Where's he off to now?"

"Bristol, apparently." She tucked her handkerchief back in her reticule and schooled her lovely face to a look of acceptance. "Business, of course. He indicated that he would be gone no more than a week."

"A week! There's very little business one could take more than a day to conclude in Bristol, I swear." He tried to erase the frown from his brow, taking his sister's arm and twining it once again with his. "No matter. I've seen how proud he is of his son, Emily. You mustn't fret at his absence. How is the babe?"

"Thriving." She sighed, but a rueful smile peeped out. "I was about to take Frederickson to see the baby, Hugh, when he tried to kiss me. Really, a new mama! What could he have been thinking of?"

"Heaven knows. I'll have a word with him."

"No, truly, that won't be necessary. He did not at all like being slapped."

"I daresay. I shouldn't myself."

"Just as well Holmsly is away," she said philosophically. "By the time he returns, it will all be forgotten, I daresay. But you were going to tell me about Miss Longstreet's young companion."

"So I was." Sir Hugh took a moment to collect his thoughts before continuing. "I very much fear that Miss

Armstrong may be in a way to edging me out of my supposed inheritance."

Emily halted abruptly, her gaze flying up to his very serious countenance. "Surely not! Why, it was decided eons ago that you were to be her heir."

"Yes, but these arrangements can be changed, my dear. She is not obliged to leave me her fortune—any more than she is obliged to stick her spoon in the wall anytime soon for my convenience."

"Oh, treacherous!" his sister pronounced. "She knows you have expectations from her. Are you quite certain, Hugh?"

"No." His thoughtful frown furrowed what Emily had once declared his "noble brow." "There is no knowing what's afoot—especially with my godmother. Since she has taken me in aversion, I've wondered if she might not look elsewhere to leave her worldly goods. But I would give a great deal to know if she has changed her will."

"Then, I shall find out for you," Emily declared. "I shall insinuate myself into her household. You know that no one is able to resist Walter. I shall take him to visit her tomorrow morning—he's at his best in the morning—and become fast friends with Miss Armstrong. See if I don't. And then I shall quiz her, in a most subtle and delicate way, until I have gathered all the information you require, my dear."

"Subtle? Delicate? These are words I never expected to hear fall from your lips, my fantastical sister. I trust you will do no such thing. The poor girl is in need of someone to befriend her, not an avenging inquisitor."

"I can see no reason to befriend her when she's attempting to do you out of your inheritance!"

Sir Hugh grimaced. "My dear Emily, anyone who has managed to suffer with Miss Longstreet for ten years is deserving of everything she may lay claim to. I don't say that the girl has any intention of becoming Miss Longstreet's heir, just that I would not be at all surprised if she were. It would delight my godmother to have sufficient reason—in her own mind—to disinherit me. My being a grown man was perhaps not quite as adequate an excuse as she would have liked."

"Miserable old sourpuss! Well, I am not a man, and Walter is but an infant, so we shall introduce ourselves into their household and learn the whole. See if we don't!"

"You terrify me," he objected, but with an amused shake of his head. "Still, I suppose it could do no harm if you were to make a morning call, Emily. I very much fear that Miss Longstreet intends to keep her companion pretty closely tied to her. You would be doing a good deed to rescue the girl from my godmother for an hour or two."

Emily nodded conspiratorially. "You're right. She's much more likely to let her tongue wag if she's not in the presence of that old ogre. Trust me, Hugh."

"God help us," he sighed, and turned the subject.

It was Aunt Longstreet's habit to get to the Pump Room early. Mostly, Nell believed, because she wished to see as few people as possible. Her aunt drank the required two glasses of water with little sign of enjoyment, and then usually urged her companion away as quickly as possible. The day after their disastrous trip to the library, Aunt Longstreet professed an interest in the Abbey Churchyard, which aroused Nell's suspicions. Aunt Longstreet was not, despite her avowed interest in tradition, much given to scouting out churches and abbeys.

While they awaited a break in the constant stream of carriages and carts, they were approached by a young man who looked vaguely familiar to Nell. He tipped his curly beaver hat to them and offered to see them safely across the road.

"Do you take us for a pair of ninnyhammers, sir?" Aunt Longstreet demanded.

"Not at all, ma'am," he assured her, the color rising in his cheeks. "But I believe you may be visitors to Bath and unfamiliar with such heavy traffic as we are accustomed to from the Oxford and London roads. Perhaps I might be of some use in escorting you across."

"I cannot see how," Aunt Longstreet grumbled. "Unless, of course, you were willing to rush out in front of a carriage and be run over. That would probably stop 'em."

"Aunt!" Nell protested. Turning to the young man, she said, "Thank you, sir. We had best simply wait for a break in the traffic, I think."

He smiled at her, and bowed, and went on his way.

Only then did Nell realize that he was the young librarian from the previous day. She sighed in despair at her aunt behaving so badly to him not once now, but twice. Really, it was too bad of her.

When at length the two women managed to cross the road, Nell was not surprised to find her aunt giving the Abbey Churchyard short shrift. "Very nice, very nice," the older woman muttered as she plodded past the magnificent stone edifice with its delightful stained-glass windows. With each step Aunt Longstreet poked her cane at the pavement as though she intended to punish it for any difficulties she found in walking. Despite the effort her niece knew it to be, she continued past the abbey and on to the Orange Grove, pausing only briefly before turning toward the Grand Parade overlooking the Parade Gardens.

"Perhaps we should find a sedan chair for you, Aunt Longstreet," Nell suggested diffidently. "We've come rather far afield."

"Nonsense. I'm perfectly capable of walking a few blocks. Does my constitution good."

Yet in fact Nell could see that her aunt was flagging. "Very well, but I should like to sit here on the bench for a moment to survey the gardens."

Her aunt did not object to being seated on the slatted
wooden bench, but her gaze fell on the houses nearby rather
than on the gardens. "I suppose one would have to be pretty
well to grass to afford one of those places," she said dismissively. "Can't think why anyone would want to live in Bath
the year-round. It's well enough for a month's visit, I suppose, but who could bear to hear the rattling of all those carriages and carts day after day?"

"One may become accustomed to them," Nell suggested.
"And they are lovely houses. I find the golden stone so very
warm and attractive. My guidebook says that one of these
houses belongs to the Earl of Kentforth."

"Humph!" Aunt Longstreet grumbled, but her gaze sharpened as the door of a nearby house opened and an elegant
man strode forth. "No doubt that is he right now," she
mocked.

"I shouldn't think so," Nell replied in her prosaic way.
"That man is as young as your godson, and the earl is re-
puted to be elderly. Sixty if he is a day."

"I'm sixty, and I do not consider myself elderly, young
lady."

"No, well, women age so much more gracefully than
men, don't you think?"

"No, I do not," her aunt snapped. She rose from the bench
and headed for the Grand Parade. "Come along. I have a
great desire to peek in the windows of Bath society—as I'm
sure one of your guidebooks would suggest."

Nell didn't argue with her aunt, but hastened to catch up
with the determined spinster. She was not, in fact, averse to
seeing what curtains and furniture she could spy through the
charmingly glazed windows of the houses, though she knew
that her aunt was merely ridiculing her curiosity. Since most
of the draperies were closed, even on such a glorious spring
day, there was little to see after all—except for her aunt's

surprisingly intense perusal of one of the nearer houses along the sweep of road.

"Does someone you know live here?" Nell asked, puzzled.

"I know almost no one in Bath," her aunt responded, glaring.

"And yet we have already met your godson," Nell pointed out. "What a strange coincidence that was, to encounter him in the lending library. Such a pleasant young man."

"Much you know," Aunt Longstreet grumbled. "He's like all men, untrustworthy, self-absorbed, and ramshackle."

Nell laughed. "Oh, I hardly think that can be true, ma'am. He was most accommodating, I thought. And only consider your own papa, so far as castigating all men goes—he was not the least untrustworthy or self-absorbed. And to think him ramshackle would be most impertinent."

"Yes, yes, my father was indeed a worthy gentleman. But probably only because his generation had some respect for their consequence and responsibilities." She waved an all-encompassing hand to indicate the male population of Bath. "Fellows today don't show the least dependability. Life is one long round of pleasure-seeking for the lot of them."

There was movement at the door of the house her aunt had been observing, and Aunt Longstreet immediately turned aside and started to thump off down the pavement. They heard brisk steps behind them after a few moments, and an older gentleman tipped his hat and said a pleasant "Good morning!" to them as he passed by. Aunt Longstreet had turned her head away, but Nell returned the greeting with a smile.

"You see," she said to her aunt when the walker was beyond hearing, "another gracious gentleman."

"Hah!" Her aunt squinted after the man, her hand gripped tight around the head of her cane. "You are easily duped by a kind word, Helen. Sometimes the most villainous men have a smile and a pleasantry. You must learn to be more discriminating."

"Yes, Aunt Longstreet," she said. "Shall I see if I can find you a sedan chair?"

"Certainly not! I'm quite capable of walking the few blocks to Queen Square."

Though this proved to be true, Nell could tell that her aunt had spent her burst of energy well before they arrived at their residence. As they traversed the last few yards, with Nell's pace slowed considerably to accommodate Aunt Longstreet, they observed a small procession arriving from the opposite direction. This consisted of a beautiful young woman in the most fetching bonnet Nell had ever seen, a footman in livery who was drawing a small wagon behind him, and in the wagon a child of a very young age, swathed in blankets and cap as though prepared for a snowstorm. A nursery maid trotted along behind the wagon.

The group stopped before the door of Aunt Longstreet's rented house, and the footman proceeded to ply the brass knocker. Woodbridge, their butler brought from Westmorland, answered the door almost immediately. By this time, however, the young lady had spied Nell and her aunt approaching, and she exclaimed, "Why, here they are! Miss Longstreet, you will scarce remember me, it has been so long since we met."

"Well, who are you?" Aunt Longstreet demanded, frowning. "If you know I won't remember you, why don't you offer me your name, girl?"

Startled by this bluntness, the girl blinked and said, "I was about to. I am Emily Holmsly, ma'am, your godson Hugh's sister."

"Didn't know he had a sister," she snapped.

"Now, Aunt Longstreet, of course you will remember that we received word of Miss Emily's marriage to Mr. Holmsly almost two years ago now." Nell offered a hand to the young woman. "How do you do, Mrs. Holmsly? We had the great pleasure of meeting your brother yesterday."

"Pleasure! Bah!" Aunt Longstreet muttered as she allowed Woodbridge to assist her into the house. "A pot of tea is what we need," she insisted to her niece.

Nell acknowledged this request and added to the butler, "If you would have them bring cups for three, please, Woodbridge, and some of the macaroons Cook baked yesterday."

As Mrs. Holmsly was gathering the child from its wagon and obviously intended to follow them into the house, Aunt Longstreet stared suspiciously at her. "I'm not in favor of children," she said. "Is it a boy or a girl?"

"Why, he's a boy," Mrs. Holmsly informed her, peering into her son's face with a good deal of besotted affection. "Most people can tell right away, can't they, Walter? They just get one look at your handsome face, and they know you're going to be the most wonderful, roll-and-tumble little boy, don't they?"

Aunt Longstreet grimaced. "You'll have to take him away if he cries. I can't stand crying."

Mrs. Holmsly looked helplessly at Nell, who said, "We've had a long walk, ma'am, and my aunt is a little fatigued." Her eyes hinted that there was nothing unusual in her aunt's behavior, but she did no more than offer a slight shrug. "Your child's name is Walter? What a lovely, strong name for a boy."

"We named him after my papa, you know," Emily Holmsly explained as she settled herself on the Egyptian sofa with the baby in her lap. "We might have named him after Hugh, but feared there would be some confusion eventually. My husband has no opinion of handing down his own name to his son. There is much too great a confusion in that."

"Oh, indeed," Nell agreed, taking a seat not far from their guest.

Aunt Longstreet eyed the child with disfavor. "He seems a great deal too young to be jauntering about the city. He's bound to catch cold."

"On such a beautiful day?" Nell protested. "And bundled up as he is? Oh, I shouldn't think so."

"But then what knowledge have you of children?" her aunt demanded.

"None whatsoever," Nell admitted, unintimidated, "but he looks quite a hearty soul."

"Oh, he is!" Emily assured them. "It is not my intention to allow him to be mollycoddled, either. Taking him out into the fresh air and letting him see the world outside of his nursery are great objects with me. I have had a few disagreements with the nursery maid, mind you, but that is because she is not a progressive sort of girl. Still, she has a great deal of experience for one her age, as she was with my husband's older sister for five years."

"How comforting," Nell murmured, since her aunt looked about to say something critical. "Ah, here's our tea. I'll pour, Woodbridge."

"I should certainly hope so," Aunt Longstreet grumbled. When she was handed her cup of tea, just the way she liked it with a healthy dollop of milk and three lumps of sugar, she sat back in her chair with a sigh. Nell thought perhaps she looked a little peaked after the long excursion and took it upon herself to entertain their guest until the tea should revive her aunt a little.

Since Emily Holmsly was a frequent visitor to Bath, she had a great number of suggestions for the amusement of Miss Longstreet and her companion. Miss Longstreet paid not the least heed to her chatter. She sipped her tea noisily and thrust the cup out for a second helping when it was empty. Then, without the slightest warning, she fell asleep.

Nell only just rescued her aunt's cup in time to keep it from falling, having been distracted by the baby's excited gurgling. She wrapped a shawl about her aunt's knees and motioned to Emily to follow her into the next room, closing the door behind them.

"She was quite exhausted from our walk," Nell explained. "I offered to procure a sedan chair for her, but she wouldn't hear of it. Never mind. She'll sleep there for half an hour and wake quite refreshed."

"You take good care of her," Emily commented as she removed another layer of her baby's clothing. "She could not be an easy woman to live with."

"Oh, it's not so difficult. I've been with her for some ten years now, and we've learned to accommodate one another."

Emily looked skeptical, but said nothing further on the subject. Instead she questioned Nell about her family, or lack of it. Nell admitted that both her parents had been dead for some years, and that she'd come to Longstreet Manor at the age of fifteen ostensibly to assist in caring for Aunt Longstreet's father in his declining days. "I used to play checkers with him or read aloud for hours at a time," she said. "He was a fine old gentleman," she said. "Did you know him, Mrs. Holmsly?"

"Oh, please, call me Emily. And, yes, I did meet him once or twice, though I could not really claim an acquaintance with him. I believe he left his entire estate to Miss Longstreet. Imagine! Since he had two daughters, I should have thought he would have divided it in some manner so that you would have received your mother's share."

"My mother's parents disapproved of her marriage."

"Nonetheless, they could have provided for you," Emily insisted. "How very odd that they did not."

"It is of no consequence," Nell assured her. "I make my

home with Aunt Longstreet, and it is a very comfortable home."

Emily looked skeptical. "But she won't live forever—and what will become of you then? Oh, of course, she will leave her property to you, to be sure."

"It is my understanding," Nell said carefully, "that your brother is Aunt Longstreet's heir."

"Well, she must surely have made provisions for you, Miss Armstrong! If not out of familial bonds, then out of gratitude for your service to her."

The baby had begun to fuss, and Nell held out her arms. Without thinking, Emily entrusted little Walter to her companion and watched as Nell kissed his plump cheeks and cooed, "Who's a good boy, then? Did you like your ride in the wagon, bumping over the cobbles? I should think that would be very amusing for a little fellow like you."

"Yes, he quite likes to be taken for a ride. But, Miss Armstrong . . ."

"Nell, if you please. What a handsome boy he is! How old is he now?"

"Four months. But, Nell . . ."

"Four months! Why, I would have taken him for six, he's such a stout fellow. His papa must be very proud."

"Yes, indeed! He already has plans for when Walter is old enough to ride, and play at sports. I believe he would already be keeping his eyes open for a pony if he weren't constantly reminded that it will be years before Walter is ready to ride. But, Nell . . ."

"Well, years pass very quickly. In just a few months he'll be crawling, and then walking, and before long he will indeed to be ready for his first pony. I am very fond of riding myself, though I did not learn until I came to Longstreet Manor. But I believe the younger one starts, the more at ease one is in the saddle. No doubt you rode early yourself, Emily?"

"I did. Papa said that I insisted on his taking me up on horseback with him when I was only five. And Hugh! The legend at Fallings is that Hugh took to riding Papa's Great Dane when he was only two. But then, Hugh is a complete hand and always has been."

Baby Walter had begun to squirm in Nell's arms, and she was unable to sufficiently calm him to keep his little voice from rising. Emily glanced at the doorway into the other room and grimaced. "I'd best be getting along, then, before your aunt awakens. It was such a pleasure to meet you, Nell. I hope we shall become better acquainted in the days to come."

"Bath seems quite a small town. No doubt we shall see you in the Pump Room one of these mornings."

"Or at one of the assemblies," Emily suggested.

Nell smiled but made no response as she helped Emily wrap the child in another layer of blankets.

"You do go to the assemblies, do you not?" Emily persisted.

"Not as yet. We've only been in town for a week, and Aunt Longstreet would find little pleasure in such entertainment."

"Then, you must come with me!"

"That's very kind of you, Emily, but I don't believe that would be possible."

"Whyever not?" her visitor demanded, but as Walter was now in full voice, she was distracted enough to allow Nell to shepherd her toward the entry hall. "I shall come again, probably without the baby," Emily announced as Woodbridge held the front door open for her.

The nursery maid stepped forward to take charge of the clamoring infant, and Emily was able to extend her hand to Nell. "Do come to call on me, in the Circus. And . . . and bring your aunt, of course. You will be most welcome."

"Thank you." Nell stood watching as her guest skipped

down the step and onto the pavement, but sighed with relief when Woodbridge closed the door on the infant's cries. "If only my aunt may still be asleep . . ."

"Helen! What's that racket?" called Aunt Longstreet from the front parlor. "Surely you've gotten rid of that tiresome girl by now."

Nell rolled her eyes skyward and went to calm her aunt.

Chapter Three

Sir Hugh was unaware that his sister had paid a call on the two Queen Square ladies when he arrived at their house. He had a good excuse for calling on them, as he juggled the unwieldy volumes of the Peerage in his arms, perfectly aware that the burden was disordering the set of his mulberry coat. No sacrifice, he assured himself ruefully, was too great to attempt to put himself into his godmother's good graces once again.

He might have saved his efforts.

Miss Longstreet regarded him with astonishment when he arrived in her parlor bearing his gift. "What the devil have you got there?" she demanded.

Her companion rose swiftly to her feet and came forward to save one of the volumes from sliding out of his arms. Sir Hugh triumphantly set the others down on a table hastily cleared by the young woman. "The current Peerage, ma'am."

"And what do you expect me to do with them, young man?"

"Why, you were quite determined yesterday in the lending library to borrow them and bring them home with you. I thought to make your task easier by bringing them straight away."

"All of them? Why would I need all of them?"

Sir Hugh felt decidedly aggrieved. "Not knowing what

your research involved, I could not very well choose a particular volume, ma'am. Perhaps you would like me to carry
off those which do not interest you?"

Miss Longstreet's countenance took on a crafty expression, and she snapped, "That's none of your business. But I
won't have them in here—nasty, dusty old books."

"I assure you they are the current edition, and unlikely to
be the least bit dusty."

"No, no, of course they aren't." Miss Armstrong wished
she could fan herself to subdue the color that she could feel
suffusing her cheeks. Her aunt's handsome godson had
come back to see them after all! Just when she'd quite made
up her mind she'd never see him again! She started toward
the pile of books. "I'll take these into the study, shall I, Aunt
Longstreet?"

"You may put them in the kitchens, for all I care," that
curmudgeonly lady retorted.

"Let me," Sir Hugh insisted as he once again gathered the
volumes in his arms.

Nell led him down the hall to a room on the left, whose
door she pushed open with a certain reluctance. "The thing
is, you see, that we have taken the house furnished, and I
should very much dislike having your volumes lost among
those of the owner." She hastened into the room and swept
a small stack of leather-bound books from the large central
table and onto a high stool that stood near it. "I will do my
utmost to see that they are well cared for, Sir Hugh, and that
they are returned to you in good time."

"There's not the least need for any speedy return of them.
I believe I ordered them when my sister's child was born,
just curious as to one branch of his ancestry, don't you
know."

"We met your sister and little Walter this morning."

"Did you? Where?"

"Why, here. She came to call."

"Did she, by God!" Sir Hugh flushed. "Begging your pardon, Miss Armstrong. I hope she was not impertinent."

"Now, why should you think that?" Nell closed the study door behind them. "Aunt Longstreet was a trifle overbearing, I fear, and your sister is not accustomed to her ways."

Sir Hugh paused in the hallway, his gaze intent on the young woman's face. "Emily can be—ah—curious to the point of incivility at times. I trust you will not allow her to browbeat you in any way."

"Your sister is charming, Sir Hugh. And the baby is delightful. Did you know that she transports him about in a wagon? How very clever of her." Feeling a bit breathless, Nell reached for the doorknob to the parlor door, but Sir Hugh stayed her hand. Her breathing stopped altogether.

"A moment. You alarm me by your evasiveness, Miss Armstrong. I suspect that my sister offended you, and I am very sorry for it."

His insistent manner startled her from her preoccupation with his physical nearness. With her gaze fully on his, she said, "You needn't be, for Mrs. Holmsly did not offend me in any way. Perhaps it is my own reserved manners which are confounding you, Sir Hugh. I am a solitary person by nature and not given to confidences. You must not read so much into my discretion."

"Now I am even more concerned," he insisted, his brows drawing down into a full-blown frown. "Trust me to have a word with my sister, ma'am. I assure you she means not the least harm."

"Truly, I am well aware of that, Sir Hugh." She reached again for the doorknob, and this time grasped and turned it, now quite unaffected by his being partially in her way. "There is no need for you to distress yourself, I assure you."

Sir Hugh left Queen Square feeling he had handled the moment awkwardly. From being rather delightfully flustered and charming, Nell had reverted completely to the reserved manner she'd attributed to herself. He walked rapidly up to the Circus and, gaining admittance to his sister's home, learned that she was not in. "And Mr. Holmsly?" he asked, forgetting his sister's grievance.

"Mr. Holmsly is out of town for a few days, Sir Hugh. Did you wish to leave a message for my mistress?"

"No, thank you. I believe I'm dining here tonight. Just tell Mrs. Holmsly that I called."

When he found himself once again standing on the pavement, Sir Hugh experienced an unfamiliar restlessness. He did not consider himself a spoiled fellow, though he certainly indulged himself as any young man of fashion did. Pursuing a course of pleasure was almost a requirement for one of his situation, and Sir Hugh enjoyed riding, driving, and gaming as much as the next man.

Because of his expectations from his godmother, he had never seriously concerned himself with the potential danger of his current difficulties. His father, a bluff and hearty man, had been given to excessive gambling, and he was not a consistent winner at the tables. In fact, Sir Walter had left Fallings encumbered to a degree that had alarmed Hugh when he learned, only on his father's death, where matters stood. But he had been comforted by the knowledge that with good management and a reasonable amount of care, nothing financially disastrous was likely to happen.

Perhaps all along it had been the knowledge that in time there would be Miss Longstreet's property to help restore the family's fortunes, which had bolstered Sir Hugh's confidence. Because now, when for the first time he felt less than sure of that eventual inheritance, he found himself taking another look at his situation—and finding it worrisome.

"What ho, old man!" a voice called to him, interrupting his cogitations. "Looks like you've lost your last friend. Nothing amiss with Mrs. Holmsly, I trust."

Sir Hugh quickly replaced his frown with a convivial

smile. "Nothing whatsoever, Hopkins. In fact, I believe she is in rare form, though she wasn't at home just now."

"Never knew anyone like Emily," his friend confessed, giving his walking stick a flamboyant twirl. "Gad, I wish she hadn't been snapped up so quickly. Might have had a try for her myself."

Sir Hugh regarded Hopkins with undisguised suspicion. "Since when have you gotten into the petticoat line?"

"Well, I'm not, in the ordinary way of things, but your sister makes a man reconsider."

"Consider yourself lucky," Sir Hugh muttered. "She'd have led you a merry dance."

"I daresay"—Hopkins grinned at the baronet—"but that's a deal more interesting than finding oneself leg-shackled to some prissy miss who wants to spend the rest of her life keeping house in the country!"

"Truly a fate worse than death," agreed Sir Hugh. "Where are you headed, Hopkins?"

"Thought I'd take a look at Parton's new pair. Did you hear he won them from Lord Westwick?"

Sir Hugh's brows rose. "When did this happen?"

"Night before last. Some deep play at one of those cozy gaming houses in George Street. You've probably been there—a Mrs. Borman's."

The baronet shook his head. "Not that I recall. Westwick seems to have lost his rudder since his wife died. He's only just out of mourning, isn't he?"

"Not something I keep track of," Hopkins admitted. "But, now you mention it, he has been behaving oddly. Thought it was just his age."

"He can't be much above sixty."

"I should live so long! Probably too old to be handling those grays, anyway."

Sir Hugh shook his head in disagreement. "He's as spry as you are, my friend, at twice your age. I watched him

guide that pair through a very sticky set of circumstances
not two months ago. Very clever and skilled, indeed."

"If you say so. Don't really know the man myself. But
Parton won the grays right and tight. He had all the cards
that night. And Westwick was a bit foxed, if you ask me."

"Too bad. I think he bred the grays himself."

"Well, are you coming with me or not?" Hopkins asked,
impatient to be off.

Sir Hugh would have enjoyed the diversion, but he was
not particularly fond of Parton. Seeing the grays in his pos-
session would do nothing to uplift his spirits. "I have business at home. Another time."

"Can't think why you should put business before pleasure, my dear fellow," complained Hopkins. "Happen I'll
see you later at the rooms."

"No doubt. Emily has insisted on my escorting her."

Hopkins grinned. "Famous. Ask her to save a set for me."

"Oh, no. You'll have to ask her yourself when we get
there."

"A lot of help you are," Hopkins grumbled as he strolled
off toward town.

Despite Emily's earlier instructions via a much under-
scored note to her brother, she was not dressed for an
evening out at the ballroom when Sir Hugh arrived for dinner. He raised his brows at the decorousness of her gown—
a short tunic of white crepe over green sarcenet—as he
raised her hand to his lips. "Charming, my dear Emily, but
hardly what I expected to see you wearing. Are we not ad-
journing to the assembly rooms?"

"I hadn't a moment to send you a note, Hugh. Forgive
me!"

"But you did send me a note, Emily. And it very emphat-
ically informed me that I was to escort you out this
evening."

"No, I meant a second note. You see, Hugh, I ran into Lord Westwick this afternoon and have invited him to dine with us."

"Westwick? Hopkins was just speaking of him—lost his grays in a bet, I understand."

"I think it was disgraceful of Mr. Parton to take such advantage of him," his sister said, giving a decided toss to her dark curls. "The poor man is still terribly bereaved."

"Then, perhaps he shouldn't have been gambling, my dear."

"Depend upon it, Parton is to blame. I haven't the slightest doubt. Do you know the man, Hugh? He's a very disagreeable fellow, and ugly to boot."

Sir Hugh regarded his sister with amusement. "Well, he is certainly deserving of your censure if he is ugly, Emily. How dare he?"

"Oh, pooh. You know what I mean. He sneers and smirks and acts as though he's king of the world."

"A very irritating habit, I admit." He narrowed his eyes at her. "Your inviting Westwick to dine did not perhaps involve my assisting him in any way to regain his pair, did it, Emily?"

"No, no, of course not. That is hardly your responsibility." Emily seated herself on the edge of a fragile chair, clasped her hands together, and bent toward him. "I have a plan."

"Oh, God. Spare me, my dearest sister. You know very well what straits your plans have always led you into."

"No! How can you say so? Why, only last year I devised the cleverest scheme for enticing Anna's nursery maid away from her, and it has worked admirably. You've met the girl. She's wonderful with Walter."

"Indeed! Well, if it's a plan for acquiring domestic help, I hardly believe I am the one in whom to confide."

Emily grimaced. "I assure you it isn't. It is a plan to recover your inheritance."

"Ah! I did not know that I'd lost it." He cocked his head at her, more interested than he had hitherto acknowledged. "Did you discover something of importance when you shamelessly invaded the enemy's territory, Emily?"

She uttered a deep, expressive sigh. "That poor girl says she believes you to be Miss Longstreet's heir."

"But you don't believe her."

"As to that, I'm not sure. Let us say that Miss Longstreet has probably never indicated a change in her plans, so Miss Armstrong is bound to believe that her aunt intends to abide by her original intention."

"You know, Emily, I fear that you must certainly have offended Miss Armstrong by your rampant curiosity. She was equivocal when I called this afternoon to take my godmother the Peerage. We have no right, you or I, to inquire into my expectations on that front."

"Perhaps not, and I wouldn't think of doing so, save that I know how important such an inheritance must be to you, with Fallings under a burden."

"That has nothing to say to the case. Miss Longstreet is entirely at liberty to dispose of her property as she sees fit. If she wishes to endow her companion, why, one cannot wonder at it."

"Oh, she's a dreadful old woman!" Emily exclaimed. "Rude and overbearing, with no appreciation of children whatsoever. She'd probably give her property to a lunatic asylum if the idea occurred to her."

Hugh laughed. "Then don't suggest it, my dear."

"I shan't. And poor Miss Armstrong. She hasn't a penny of her own to boast of."

"I thought you were convinced that her aunt intends to endow her with all her worldly goods."

His sister frowned. "She should, of course." And then she looked guilt-stricken and thrust her hands out to her brother. "Oh, Hugh, I don't mean that you shouldn't have her property.

You most certainly should. But if it comes to you, you must be certain to do something for that poor girl. How strange that her grandfather made not the slightest provision for her!"

"Yes," he said thoughtfully. "Bad blood there, between the parents and the daughter, but that is no excuse to leave one of your own without a feather to fly with."

"And, Hugh," Emily said urgently, "you will not credit this, but Miss Longstreet and her niece do not go to the assemblies at all."

"A tragedy indeed," he remarked with a sad shake of his head and a wicked gleam in his eyes. "But you know, Emily, Miss Armstrong may not care for such things. And she may not have the proper costumes."

"Oh, I never thought of that! Of course she wouldn't. It is the most provoking thing. She is so much taller than I that I cannot offer to share my gowns with her."

"I trust you wouldn't embarrass her by doing any such thing!" he protested.

"Really, Hugh, you have so little faith in me!"

The sound of the knocker reached them, and she gave a tsk of annoyance. "Dear me, Lord Westwick is here already. I fear I shall have to tell you of my plan later. Just remember not to say anything disagreeable about Miss Longstreet."

Sir Hugh regarded her with astonishment, but was prevented from replying by the advent of his sister's butler announcing her guest.

As Sir Hugh had informed his friend Hopkins such a short while ago, Lord Westwick was anything but a decrepit old man. The gentleman who entered the room was full of vigor and sharp-eyed intelligence. Not much above average height, he was yet an impressive figure with a stately bearing and easy manners. Sir Hugh could see that Lord Westwick had a fondness for Emily, for his eyes twinkled as he brought her hand to his lips.

"Enchanted, madam! How delighted I was to have your invitation. And a chance to meet Sir Hugh again," he added as he turned to the baronet. "I regret only that Mr. Holmsly is out of town."

"Yes, it is very provoking of him," Emily agreed. "But one cannot wait for him to be here; one would see no one at all!"

"My sister exaggerates," Sir Hugh interposed. "I saw Holmsly on Monday."

"Yes, I had a word with him at the Pump Room myself the other day," Lord Westwick admitted. "Capital fellow."

"So they tell me," Emily muttered. But then her good spirits revived, as they inevitably did, and she added, "After dinner, if he is awake, I will have the nursery maid bring Walter down. I don't believe you've seen our son as yet, Lord Westwick."

"No, and I should very much like to." The older man seated himself beside Emily on the red satin-covered sofa. "I don't get out and about as much as I did when Sophie was alive. She was of a much more sociable nature than I. But in her company I could become passably affable myself."

"It is most always the women who are the more sociable, I think," Emily said. "Except perhaps for Hugh's godmother. Now, there is a decidedly unsociable woman!"

Lord Westwick cocked an inquisitive brow at Sir Hugh, who found it necessary to explain. "My godmother has come to Bath, and she was not as enchanted with Emily's little son as my sister might have wished. So beware! When he is brought down, you will have to praise him to the skies to win her approbation."

"It is nothing of the sort! I do not expect everyone to find Walter as delightful as I do, but she told me I would have to remove him if he cried. Imagine!"

"Delicate nerves, no doubt," Lord Westwick suggested, but with a quiver at the corner of his mouth.

Emily appeared to consider this for a moment before she responded, "Perhaps that is it. She has, after all, had so little contact with children and is accustomed to the peaceful atmosphere of her home in the country."

Hugh could not guess what she was about, but he felt certain he would not approve if he could. And Emily was not ready to drop the subject of his godmother. She turned to his lordship in a confiding way and said, "She has lived all her life in Westmorland, with scarcely a visit to London since she became a woman. Don't you think that affects a person, living always in the country away from the sophistication and stimulation of a metropolis?"

"Not everyone wishes for either the sophistication or the stimulation," Lord Westwick said thoughtfully. "Some people appreciate the slower pace of life. They feel an attachment to the land, and enjoy the simple pleasures to be found there."

"Well, I am sure I love residing in the country, but I would be most unhappy if I were never to get to Bath or London at all! I should become dull as ditch water."

"That would not be possible," Lord Westwick informed her gallantly. "But your many admirers would be devastated if you didn't alight in town every so often."

Emily sighed. "Holmsly felt Bath would be preferable to London for a change of scene. It is not so overpowering—there is not so much noise or so many people or so much excitement. And I must admit that it is easy to get everywhere. One isn't forever calling for the carriage, except for evening entertainments. Even Hugh's godmother seems to walk everywhere, despite the hills and the traffic."

"I'm fond of walking myself," Lord Westwick said. He turned to the baronet and asked, "Do I know your godmother, Sir Hugh? She sounds an adventurous woman."

"She comes from much the same area of the country as you, Lord Westwick—Westmorland. Her name is Rosemarie Longstreet."

The earl's face underwent a decided change in color, and for a moment Sir Hugh thought that he had choked on something, though neither food nor drink were to hand. All the vivacity that had been there disappeared, and a wary, uncomfortable expression took its place. In a grave voice he said, "I do know Miss Longstreet."

Emily's mischievous grin peeked out. "Obviously you know her well," she teased.

"I don't understand," the earl replied, his tone cool.

Sir Hugh very much feared that his sister had once again taken a bold misstep. "My sister means," he offered in a soothing voice, "that my godmother is a bit of a curmudgeon. Almost anyone who encounters her comes away with a decided—ah—impression, shall we say, of her cantankerous nature."

The color began to creep back into Lord Westwick's cheeks. "I see. Well, I have not had the pleasure of encountering her for many, many years, and she was not the least bit cantankerous as a young woman." He frowned and said, "I did encounter two women in the street outside my residence this morning—a rather tall young lady and an older lady whom I confess looked familiar. I could not place them, but now I think on it, the elder lady might have been Miss Longstreet. If so, she's much changed." He frowned, abstracted.

"The young one would have been Miss Armstrong, the niece and companion," Emily said, recalling his attention.

"Margaret's daughter?"

Sir Hugh was beginning to realize that Lord Westwick knew the Longstreets very well indeed. "Yes, I believe her mother's name was Margaret. I never met her myself, for she had made an alliance of which the family did not approve, and she was banished from their family circle. But the Armstrongs have been dead for some years now, and their daughter resides with my godmother."

"I see." Lord Westwick stared down at his hands for a moment and then added, "I'm sorry to hear of Margaret's death.

I presume the elder Longstreets are gone, too. I'm afraid I haven't kept up with the news from Westmorland."

"Oh, yes. Mr. Longstreet outlived his wife, and he died several years ago," Sir Hugh said. "Is their property near yours, Lord Westwick?"

"Perhaps thirty miles distant. We all attended the same assemblies when we were young. Lord, that seems like ancient history!"

Emily looked intrigued. "Oh, do tell us what Miss Longstreet was like as a girl!"

"Not at all the curmudgeon you say she is now," he assured her. "She and her sister Margaret were pretty as pictures, especially alongside one another."

"Pretty! How very astonishing. She is all angles and wispy gray hair now. With the fiercest eyes I've seen in many a year." Emily seemed to recall herself, and added, "Sharp as a tack, you know. Nothing escapes her notice. I do love a feisty elderly lady, don't you, Lord Westwick?"

His lordship regarded her dolefully. "I'm not at all sure that I do, Mrs. Holmsly. My wife was of an entirely different nature—very agreeable and accommodating. I daresay Miss Longstreet would terrify me if I were to meet her today."

"Oh, no, no!" protested Emily. "Nothing of the sort. She is merely a fascinating character. I believe you owe it to your past acquaintance and the proximity of your properties in Westmorland to call on her here in Bath."

"Do you?" The earl turned a quizzical eye on Sir Hugh. "And you, Sir Hugh? Do you recommend that I reacquaint myself with your godmother?"

"I'm sure it is a matter of total indifference to me," said the baronet, adding firmly, "as it should be of my sister."

"How can you say so, Hugh? Poor Miss Longstreet is almost without acquaintance here in Bath. It would be unkind of his lordship not to call on her and her niece." Emily turned to Lord Westwick and said, "They're in Queen Square, you know. Quite an old-fashioned location, but they've let a charming house. I'm sure Miss Longstreet would be delighted to have you call. And perhaps you could escort them out of an evening."

Sir Hugh disapproved of this less-than-subtle attempt to manipulate the earl. "Emily, my dear, I'm sure Lord Westwick has better things to do with his time than to wait on my godmother and her niece. I myself have the intention of keeping an eye on the two ladies and seeing that they enjoy their stay in Bath."

Undaunted, Emily confided to the earl, "Unfortunately, Miss Longstreet is not overfond of my brother these days, my lord. She considers him something of a callow youth, I think. No doubt she would welcome company of her own generation."

Lord Westwick looked from one to the other of the two siblings, shook his head, and sighed. "I'll call on her," he promised. "But she will most likely refuse to see me."

Chapter Four

Nell had found her aunt slightly indisposed on the day following the visits from Sir Hugh and his sister. The indisposition was due more to an indulgence in her favorite potted viands than to anything else, as witnessed by her gout acting up most painfully. And Miss Longstreet was not an accommodating patient.

"Take it away, take it away!" Aunt Longstreet insisted when Nell tried to wrap her foot in a warm rug. "It does me not the least good, as I have told you a hundred times if I've told you once."

As it was quite true that her aunt had said this many times, Nell removed the rug, but she knew from experience that her aunt would demand its return within the hour. If Rosemarie Longstreet was cranky at the best of times, she was intolerable when her foot throbbed from the gout. But as she would not listen to reason, it was better to retreat from her vicinity.

Thus Nell disposed of the warm rug by setting it on the stool across from her aunt's chair and announced that she was going to the lending library.

"You're leaving me alone?" her companion asked in a querulous voice.

"No, I'm leaving you to the tender care of the servants," Nell told her firmly. "Mrs. Hodges is ready to be of service at the slightest ring of the bell, which I have put on the table right next to your chair."

"Oh, the servants," her aunt said dismissively. "There's probably not a one of them in the house."

"I assure you that there is, including your dressing woman." Nell picked up her paisley shawl and draped it around her shoulders. "It's too fine a day for me to stay indoors. I shall find you a book at the lending library, and perhaps I will even bring you back a ginger biscuit from the pastry cook's."

"I pray you will not put yourself to so much bother," Aunt Longstreet sniffed.

Nell laughed and patted her aunt's cheek. "It is no bother at all, my dear. You'll be more comfortable without me hovering over you."

"That is certainly true."

On her way out of the house, Nell consulted briefly with the housekeeper, accepting a basket that good woman handed her, and a list of necessities. While Nell would not have hesitated for a moment to take off with a basket over her arm in the country, she did just feel a twinge of discomfort about doing so in Bath. It occurred to her that she had seen no one else strolling about the sophisticated streets of the town with a basket on her arm. She would look very provincial indeed!

But looking provincial was not the worst fate she could endure, Nell decided as she escaped from the stuffy town house. Aunt Longstreet insisted in keeping the rooms overly warm for such a springlike day, and it was delightful for Nell to find herself in the fresh morning air scented by new growth. Stretching her long legs, she set a good pace down the square and across the maze of streets to Milsom. Unfortunately, she found it was too early for the library to be open, so she indulged herself in gazing in the windows of the shops along the street.

If I had a spare guinea, she thought, I would most decidedly purchase that beaded reticule or perhaps the pink slippers. The fact that she had nowhere to wear such items bothered her not in the least. It was merely a game she played, even at the country store where she shopped when in Westmorland. Nell liked pretty things, as her mother had. Margaret Armstrong's disastrous marriage had made it necessary for her, over the course of Nell's early life, to dispose of the jewelry she had brought from her home.

Each time a piece had to be sold, she would fondle it for a day or two, telling the young Nell how her papa had given it to her at her come-out, or her mama had ordered it specially for this birthday, or her sister had passed on one of her own less favored items. Margaret would pin the brooch to Nell's apron, or let the necklace rest around her neck for a while. "Someday you'll have jewelry of your own," she had assured the girl. "Unless, of course, you are as imprudent as I, and marry for love!"

But her parents' marriage, as imprudent as it had proved financially, had been quite wonderful in other ways. Her father and mother had cared deeply for one another, and had been physically demonstrative all Nell's life. They had become so accustomed to kissing and touching during the many years they'd spent together before Nell's arrival, that they were unable to substantially modify their pattern. Having witnessed that emotional and physical satisfaction, Nell longed to know the intimacy of such a relationship herself.

But she understood that she would not marry at all. Her promise to her grandfather on his deathbed was as compelling to her today as it had been at the time. One did not promise a dying man that one would stay with his daughter and take care of her, only to turn around and marry the first man who asked.

There would come a day, of course, when Aunt Longstreet died, but Nell did not delude herself that that day would arrive before Nell became a confirmed spinster, far too old to marry and bear children. And even if her aunt

were to die soon, Nell's lack of a dowry would prevent anyone from being interested in her. Aunt Longstreet might provide some small legacy for Nell in her will if she wished, but
her grandfather, as well as Aunt Longstreet, had made it
clear to her that Longstreet Manor was destined for Sir
Hugh.

Because her aunt was tight with a penny, Nell received an
allowance which scarcely stretched to replacing worn-out
gloves and gowns. There was little chance that she would
manage to set aside much for her own old age. And nothing
at all if she chose to purchase such fripperies as a beaded
reticule, Nell thought with wry amusement.

Down the street she became aware of a young man un-
locking the door of the lending library, and she turned in that
direction to complete her errand. Finding Aunt Longstreet a
book that would hold her attention was no easy task. As Nell
approached, she realized it was the same young man who
had spoken to them the previous day and whom her aunt had
now browbeaten on two separate occasions. If he had not already caught sight of her, Nell thought perhaps she would
have chosen to retreat.

But he had not only seen her, he was smiling broadly and
offered an extravagant bow. "Your servant, ma'am. I see that
you are unaccompanied by your aunt. I trust she is well."

"Not so very plump today," Nell admitted, smiling in return. "My aunt suffers from the gout and is here to take the
waters."

"There are those who swear by them," he said, though he
sounded rather skeptical.

"You are not one of them, I gather."

He shrugged. "I doubt they do anyone any harm, but I
have yet to see with my own eyes anyone who has greatly
benefited from them. Won't you step inside, Miss . . ."

"Armstrong. Thank you."

"Richard Bentley, at your service."

Nell preceded him into the dim interior of the lending library. The vast room looked different without the usual crowd of patrons. Like the study in their rented house on Queen Square, leather-bound volumes filled shelf after shelf. There were also rows of marbled-board-covered books closer to hand, the ones most library patrons would be searching for. Mr. Bentley waved a hand at the closest shelves and said, "Our most recent acquisitions, Miss Armstrong. Perhaps one of them would interest you."

"Probably," she admitted with a chuckle, "but I'm here today looking for something for my aunt."

"Ah, yes, that good woman was interested in the Peerage, I believe. You know, they change very little from year to year. I cannot believe she would find last year's entries on any given person so different from this year's. Perhaps you could . . ."

"My aunt has been supplied with a complete set of the newest Peerage, thank you. What I had in mind was something more lively. But not frivolous! And nothing like sermons or edifying essays, either. She is not an easy woman to choose a title for."

"I can well believe it," he said with a perfectly straight face. "Let me think a moment."

He wandered off in what appeared to be a purposeless manner, but soon was picking up and replacing volumes from a variety of locations. A very few of them he kept in his hands, and at length he motioned Nell over to the counter where he placed them for her perusal.

"A volume of poetry by Cowper rather than Lord Byron might be more appealing to a person of conservative taste. Or perhaps this history of Elizabethan times. Or this novel by Mr. Sterne. Quite a few of our patrons find his work to their liking. If your aunt perhaps does read contemporary novels, she might appreciate this one by 'a Lady,' which is most amusing."

Mr. Bentley continued through the volumes he'd chosen, offering a word of praise or explanation as he went. Nell could not help but notice that the librarian was a good deal taller than she (a very rare circumstance), and a rather handsome man, too. He had black hair more closely trimmed than was the fashion of the day, and his eyes were a rich and eloquent brown. It seemed to Nell, though she was willing to consider that she was fooling herself, that he (for some inexplicable reason) admired her. His gaze was intent, his smile warm, his interest keen. He even dared to allow his hand to lightly brush hers as he passed a volume across. She almost smiled, pleased to note she felt none of the disconcerting effects of a similar familiarity the previous day. She was not becoming a susceptible ninny after all!

When she had settled on two of the books he had suggested, he added, "There is a particular title which I believe your aunt would enjoy, but it was recently borrowed and will likely not be available for a day or two. If you would permit me to let you know when it is returned . . ."

"That's exceedingly kind of you. I'm certain to come by every few days, and if you were to put it aside . . ."

"Yes, yes. That is what I shall do."

By this time several other patrons had entered the circulating library. One man was approaching the counter with a determined scowl upon his countenance. Nell gave Mr. Bentley a commiserating grin, thanked him for his assistance, and gathered up her books. She had intended to find something for herself to read, but decided that she had spent quite enough time here for one morning. So she tucked the books into her basket and made her way once again out into the lovely spring morning.

Because Nell was a daydreamer, she easily drifted into romantic thoughts as she strolled along Milsom Street. She pictured herself walking alongside a man, his tall, straight figure overshadowing her own. Or they would be walking in the country, by a stream, with birds twittering. And her companion would have a volume of poetry with him—Lord Byron's—which he would open as they seated themselves on the bank of the stream. His voice, deep and melodious, would enthrall her as he read poems of love and gallantry.

Her companion in this daydream should have been Mr. Bentley. And at first she had thought that it was. But as she lifted her modestly lowered eyes to meet his—it was Sir Hugh who smiled across at her.

Lordy, that would never do, Nell scolded herself. Way above her touch! Mr. Bentley, at least, seemed to be of a station not dissimilar from her own, given that she was more companion than niece to her aunt. And, crotchety as her aunt was, the older woman had a point about men. They could be unreliable and thoughtless, even the best of them. Nell had to look no further than her own father and grandfather to see that.

She paused in the door of a chemist's shop, allowing her eyes to adjust from the sunlight to the gloom within. Three of the items on Mrs. Hodges' list were to be found here, so she stepped briskly into the store, allowing her daydream to evaporate like the morning mist.

By the time Nell returned to the house in Queen Square, she had accumulated quite a few items in her basket. She had taken her time, enjoying the spring sunlight and the delightful breeze that tossed her ringlets in a decidedly playful manner. It was the kind of day that she especially enjoyed at Longstreet Manor, where she would escape onto the brick pathways beyond the kitchen garden, eventually losing herself in the home wood and returning with an armful of early spring blossoms.

Bath offered its own pleasures on such a day, and Nell arrived back in excellent spirits. She had scarcely set her basket down on the table in the entry hall when she heard her aunt's voice raised in indignation.

"You cannot seriously expect me to welcome you into my house, sir! Who the devil is Mrs. Holmsly, and what does she have to say to anything?"

The footman who had opened the door to Nell remarked with an impassive face, "A gentleman has called, miss. His card is on the salver."

Nell's heart beat more quickly as she picked up the card that lay there. But she was astonished to see that her aunt's caller was Lord Westwick. Not that Nell had ever heard of Lord Westwick, but it astonished her that her aunt knew anyone of such a high rank as an earl. Nell was tempted, given the rancor in her aunt's voice, to disappear into the nether reaches of the house, but thought better of such a scheme. Her primary duty, in her own mind, was to act as intermediary between her aunt and the rest of the world, since Aunt Longstreet was obviously incapable of behaving in a fashion acceptable to anyone but herself.

Straightening her shoulders and pasting a polite smile on her countenance, she let herself into the parlor as though nothing were afoot. Fortunately she remembered to bring with her the two books Mr. Bentley had urged upon her at the library, so she had an excuse at hand for invading her aunt's presence.

A very distinguished gentleman stood across the room from Aunt Longstreet, who sat upright in her chair, glaring at him. Lord Westwick had silver hair and was dressed in a coat that had obviously been made by a very skilled tailor. In fact, every item of his dress suggested that he was *au courant* with the fashions of the day. His neckcloth was a veritable waterfall of fine white linen. Nell dropped a curtsy to him.

"I beg your pardon for interrupting, Aunt Longstreet. I have brought you some books from the library, but I could return later with them."

The gentleman made her a formal bow, as Rosemarie

Longstreet barked out an introduction, "This is Lord West-wick, Helen. Sir, my niece, Helen Armstrong."

"How do you do, Miss Armstrong?" his lordship mur-mured. "Please don't leave on my account. I was about to depart myself."

"Not until you explain why you have come!" Miss Longstreet insisted.

Lord Westwick looked ruefully at Nell and said, "I had dinner last evening with Mrs. Holmsly and her brother, Sir Hugh Nowlin, your godson. Mrs. Holmsly mentioned that you were in Bath, and realizing that we must in some kind be neighbors, both coming from Westmorland, suggested that I call on you, as you had settled in Queen Square for some time."

"Busybody!" Aunt Longstreet declared. "Had the imper-tinence to call on me with her screaming child just yester-day."

"He was not screaming, Aunt," Nell reminded her exag-gerating relative. "Won't you sit down, Lord Westwick? Could I ring for tea?"

"No, you could not!" her aunt interposed. "Lord West-wick is leaving!"

"Just so," he agreed, but Nell noticed the rueful light in his eyes, which made her take an immediate liking to him.

"I shall see you out, then," she said, and ignored her aunt's disparaging comment that this "would not be at all necessary."

In the hall with the door shut behind them, Nell turned to their visitor with an apologetic smile. "My aunt is indis-posed this morning, and therefore a little out of sorts. I pray you will disregard her crotchets. Perhaps if you were to call on another occasion . . ."

"I'm not sure I'm brave enough to beard the lion in her den twice," he admitted. "You're Margaret's daughter?"

"Yes. Did you know my mother?"

"I did. A beautiful, spirited girl she was when I knew her, many years ago. I was sorry to hear that she and your father were both gone. And your grandparents, too. How sad for you."

"Well, it was long ago," Nell said bracingly. "And I still have my aunt—as you see."

"Yes," he agreed with a shake of his head, "you most certainly do. I should like to hear more of your mother on another occasion. Would it be acceptable for me to call on you sometime?"

"Of course. And don't be put off by my aunt. On another occasion she will probably welcome you with open arms."

"Oh, I very much doubt that. But I shall come again."

He bowed to her, accepted his hat from the footman, and strode purposefully down the steps to the pavement. Nell watched him leave with a puzzled expression. If he had known her mother, then he had no doubt known Aunt Longstreet, too, when she was a girl. How odd that Aunt Longstreet had been so impossibly rude to him. Nell shrugged and picked up the basket to deliver her purchases to the housekeeper. There was no understanding Aunt Longstreet.

Sir Hugh avoided visiting his godmother for several days. In part this was because he wished to have no role in his sister's plans with regard to his godmother, and in part it was because he still didn't know what those plans were. After Lord Westwick had made his surprising statement that Miss Longstreet would most likely refuse to see him, dinner had been announced, and the opportunity to seek an explanation had been lost.

Though Emily, too, had obviously been startled, she was not the least bit forthcoming when their guest had departed and her brother had pressed her for details of her plan to restore his fortunes.

"No, no. I shall say no more on that head," she had declared, making a pretty moue with her mouth. "I may have misjudged his lordship, or your godmother, and I shall not embarrass myself by pursuing that avenue."

Though Sir Hugh did not for a moment trust that Emily would mind her own business, he did believe that she had had something of a comeuppance with regard to Lord Westwick. He could only hope that she would turn her very creative mind to some other project than his inheritance—or lack of it. In the interests of being out of sight and out of mind, he made himself scarce not only in Queen Square, but at the Holmslys as well.

So it was more than a week before he came across his sister again, and this time their meeting occurred in the hot, and very crowded, upper assembly rooms. Sir Hugh was pleased to see that Holmsly accompanied his wife on this occasion, though he detected a slight air of tension in Holmsly's frown when Emily was claimed by one of her cicisbeos. Emily's haughty expression in response to this did not bode well for marital felicity, in Sir Hugh's opinion. But then Sir Hugh had no experience of the matter, he reminded himself.

"Well, John, returned from the wilds of Bristol, are you?" he offered pleasantly as he came abreast of his brother-in-law.

"Some days ago," Holmsly said shortly. "Why is it that your sister must be forever dancing with some rakehell, Hugh?"

Sir Hugh regarded his brother-in-law with patent amusement. "I should think it is because one is forever asking her, John. It would be rude of her to refuse for no other reason than that you would like her to stay by your side."

"I have no objection to her dancing. It is the type of man she dances with that I object to. Why couldn't someone like Figby over there ask her to dance?"

Hugh lifted his quizzing glass and gazed in the direction

Holmsly indicated. Across the room stood a very short, rumpled individual who blinked repeatedly at his companion, an aging dowager in a puce gown. "I should think Emily would terrify such a man, John," he remarked.

His brother-in-law laughed. "Yes, I daresay she would. Pity she doesn't terrify the likes of Mannering."

As Emily's partner, Giles Mannering, was a close associate of Hugh's, this comment could hardly be ignored. "Mannering is hardly what I would call a rakehell, John. Granted, he will flatter my sister outrageously, but he has very refined manners and is unlikely to discompose her in any way. I thought you brought her to town so that she might enjoy herself."

"So I did," Holmsly grudgingly admitted, running a hand through his thick brown locks. "But I could wish she didn't enjoy herself quite so much with all these man milliners and gazetted flirts."

Hugh allowed a moment to pass before he remarked, "She misses you when you're away, you know. There may be an element of retaliation in her choice of partners."

Holmsly frowned at him, and his lips tightened slightly. "I am never from home except when business requires it. Your sister cannot believe otherwise."

"Ah, who knows what goes through the mind of a woman," Hugh said. "I've known Emily all her life, and I certainly cannot guess the half of what goes on in her mind."

Holmsly chuckled. "How true. She's a remarkable woman, isn't she?"

Glad to see his brother-in-law restored to good humor, Hugh agreed. "Quite remarkable. When we were young . . ." His eye was suddenly caught by a surprising sight at the end of the dance floor. "My word! Is that my godmother?"

Holmsly turned to look in the direction his companion was staring. "By Jove, I believe it is! What a figure she cuts!

Haven't seen a gown like that since I was a child. And who's the chit with her?"

Hugh's eyes moved to the taller, younger companion. "Her niece, Helen Armstrong. Where did they get those gowns?"

Chapter Five

Nell had managed to ignore the odd looks she and her aunt were given until she noticed the expression on Sir Hugh's face. Though she could not be unaware of the difference between the heavy rich fabrics that she and Aunt Longstreet wore, and the flimsy, insubstantial materials the ladies around her sported, Nell had, on the whole, convinced herself that, for such a luxurious occasion as an assembly in Bath, their own gowns were surely more appropriate.

The startled—nay, shocked would not be too strong a term—expression on the baronet's face gave the lie to this reasoning. Nell felt a flush creep into her cheeks. She had never before been to an assembly in either Westmorland or Bath, and she had been filled with a kind of exuberant excitement when Aunt Longstreet announced that they were to go. Though she had wished for it, she had not believed they would ever attend such an occasion. Her aunt had admitted—to Nell's astonishment—that she had caused several of her old gowns to be packed in their trunks. Since her relation's height and spare figure were close enough to her own configuration, Nell had been relieved to hear that they would have something unexceptionable to wear.

Now it appeared that the heavy satin gown she wore, such a lovely rich burgundy color, with acres of blonde lace, was not acceptable to the gathered gentry. She raised her head a little higher, making her no doubt the tallest woman in the room (especially with the exotic confection that adorned her head). What did it matter, after all, if she and Aunt Longstreet were not dressed in the fashion of the day? Fashion was a fleeting thing, when all was said and done, and its pursuit not something that a serious-minded young woman should pride herself upon.

Or so she attempted to tell herself, her color high, as she surreptitiously watched the baronet approach them from across the crowded room.

Sir Hugh made his bow to her aunt, graciously including her in his greeting. "Miss Longstreet, Miss Armstrong. I am enchanted to find you here. Had I known of your intention of attending an assembly, I would have been honored to offer myself as your escort."

"We didn't need your escort," Aunt Longstreet snapped. "We are perfectly capable of getting ourselves from Queen Square to the Upper Rooms."

"So I see." Sir Hugh glanced around briefly, as though to satisfy himself that they had not, in fact, come with an escort. He lowered his voice to say, "It is, however, customary for ladies alone at night to be attended by a male escort. I would prefer it in future if you would call upon me for that service."

"You would prefer it?" Aunt Longstreet sputtered. "What the devil does that have to say to anything? I shall do precisely as I choose."

There was steel in his voice when he replied, "I certainly hope you will think better of that decision, ma'am. I should not like to think of your being accosted on the streets of Bath because you were without an escort."

"We had the footman," she retorted, defiant. "We had no need for another."

"Ah, but I think you did," he said, his tone smooth and his voice not carrying beyond their little trio. "I am your godson, Miss Longstreet, and it would be my pleasure—as well as my duty—to see you safely about Bath, at any time you should require my services."

Nell was surprised to see her aunt turn away from him rather than counter him with her usual invective. But there was indeed something about Sir Hugh's demeanor that was just a trifle intimidating. His will, apparently, was quite as strong as her aunt's in this matter, and he obviously had no intention of being gainsaid. He turned toward Nell with a slight smile and added, "I think you are a woman of good sense, Miss Armstrong. I trust you will call upon me in future to render you and my godmother such escort services as you may require."

"Indeed," she replied, not meeting his sharp gaze.

Nell heard his exasperated sigh and clenched her hands more firmly together. More than anything she wished to simply disappear from the face of the earth. Or at the very least to be safely at home in the parlor in Queen Square, or better yet at Longstreet Manor. To her alarm, she heard Sir Hugh say, "Perhaps you would care to join this set with me, Miss Armstrong?"

The color rose higher on her cheeks. "Oh, no. Thank you, but I could not."

"Did you not come to dance?" he inquired gently.

"No. That is . . . I have no intention of dancing."

Nell heard a little gasp beside her and turned to find Sir Hugh's sister Emily staring at her. "Whyever not?" Emily demanded. "Hugh is an exquisite dancer, Miss Armstrong."

Nell dropped a curtsy to the pretty young matron. "Oh, that does not surprise me at all, but you see I have never been to a dance before, and I have no knowledge of how to execute all those intricate steps."

"Never been to a dance before!" Emily looked truly shocked. "But that's unconscionable!"

"No, why should it be?" Nell asked. "We have come merely as observers tonight, my aunt and I. I am quite enchanted with the colors and the music and the elegance of the dancers. We were going to find ourselves chairs where we might enjoy the proceedings."

Sir Hugh, his face impassive, bowed and said, "Allow me to find seats for you."

"Yes, do make yourself of some use," Aunt Longstreet suggested, "instead of just standing there and prosing on at us."

The baronet accepted this sally without demurral. Turning to his sister, he asked, "Where are you seated, Emily? Would they have a view of the dancing from there?"

"Yes, indeed," Emily assured them. "Please, follow me."

The crowds seemed to part before Emily's determined progress. When a young gentleman attempted to stay her, she rapped his hand with her fan and exclaimed, "Not now, Whissenby! If I promised you this dance, I am very sorry, but I have a duty to perform."

And perform it she did as she presented her seats to the two visitors with a flourish of her hand. "Here! The best seats in the rooms, if I do say so myself. Holmsly is wonderful at that sort of thing. Pray be seated, and Hugh will bring you a glass of orgeat."

"I detest orgeat," Aunt Longstreet said, but she accepted the chair with some eagerness. Nell suspected that her gout was troubling her, though she had made no mention of it.

Emily remained standing at Nell's side, seeming determined to offer whatever assistance was needed. She bent down and whispered in Nell's ear, "They are only country-dances, you know. The waltz isn't danced here yet, more's the pity. Didn't you learn country-dances in the schoolroom?"

"Not in any recognizable fashion. My mama was my only teacher, and since there was no one else to form a set, it was impossible to do more than imagine what such dancing must be like."

Emily frowned. "It is shameful that your aunt never took you to an assembly. How were you to meet young men? When were you to have any fun?"

Nell laughed. "I assure you, Mrs. Holmsly . . . Emily, that I have had many very enjoyable days at Longstreet Manor."

"I cannot conceive how," Emily admitted with a disparaging glance at Aunt Longstreet, whose concentration on the scene before her was almost unnerving. "Is she looking for someone in particular?" Emily whispered to Nell.

"I don't think so. She certainly didn't mention that we were to meet anyone here. Is it true that we should not have come without an escort?"

"Most assuredly. You undoubtedly shocked the master of ceremonies, but I daresay your aunt annihilated him with one of her wicked comments."

Nell's lips twitched. "She did. She told him that she had better things to do than cater to a bunch of ill-conceived, antiquated rules."

"Ha! I should have thought anything antiquated would have pleased her excessively," Emily retorted.

At this point Sir Hugh arrived with glasses of orgeat for Nell and Emily, and wine for Aunt Longstreet. His godmother sniffed it suspiciously and took a small sip. "Watered!" she announced, but she proceeded to drink it all the same.

Emily's husband joined them and was introduced to the two women. Nell thought Mr. Holmsly cut a dashing figure, like someone from a romance—with his shining black hair, piercing blue eyes and rugged features. He was just the sort of man she imagined married to Emily, though she was a trifle disappointed when he spoke, for his conversation was somewhat prosaic—a comment on the state of the roads between Bath and Bristol.

She caught the amusement in Sir Hugh's eyes as he regarded her. "Did you think he would offer tales of high adventure?" he asked in an undertone. "Be thankful he is not as derring-do as his appearance, else he would be totally unable to manage my sister!"

"Your sister is charming."

"Yes, but quite a handful, I promise you. I don't envy Holmsly the keeping of her."

As Emily was smiling very prettily at her husband just at that moment, Nell could not conceive what difficulty Mr. Holmsly ever had with his wife, but she remained silent. There were mysteries between married couples that she would never experience. And she did not intend to pretend that she possessed some sophisticated knowledge which she did not.

Sir Hugh accepted her silence with good grace and asked, "Shall I tell you about some of the people here tonight?"

"Oh, yes, please. I should like that immensely," she said, her eyes sparkling.

"We shall start with the couple at the head of that set," he said, indicating the dancers closest to them. "Mrs. Witchford and Mr. Kennyhall. She comes to Bath for two months in the spring each year, without her husband, for the express purpose of taking the waters—and setting up a flirtation. Mr. Kennyhall is not the gentleman with whom she has set up her flirtation this year. That is Mr. Pymore, the next gentleman in the set. His partner is the youngest Haddenham daughter, the fifth. Her family is anxious to see her settled, but she has shown no inclination toward any of the young men who have shown an interest."

"She's quite lovely. But she must be very young. Surely too young to marry."

"Oh, no. All of her sisters married in their first London Seasons, at seventeen. Miss Haddenham is probably eighteen or thereabouts."

"Well, I hope she will not marry unless she finds a gentleman who suits her," Nell remarked incautiously.

Sir Hugh's brows rose. "Do you know her?"

"Not at all. I speak merely as one who believes a young woman must take responsibility for her actions, as no one is as certain to have her best interests at heart as she herself."

"I see." Sir Hugh did not look as though he "saw" at all. After a moment, however, he proceeded to run through the other dancers he was acquainted with, but he paused when they both heard Emily exclaim, "Lord Westwick! How good to see you again."

Nell's gaze flew instinctively to her aunt, who was frowning at the newcomer, her eyes narrowed to a fierce glare. This did not seem to have any effect on the earl, who raised Emily's hand to his lips with practiced grace.

"Mrs. Holmsly, how delightful to find you here. And, Miss Longstreet." He made an elaborate bow to Aunt Longstreet, who pointedly ignored him, before turning to Nell. "And, Miss Armstrong, I trust you are enjoying our Bath entertainments."

"Very much, my lord, thank you," Nell replied with her deepest curtsy.

Emily intervened to say, "This is Miss Armstrong's first assembly, Lord Westwick. I can hardly credit it! And she is not familiar with our country-dances, to say nothing of the waltz. I have been cudgeling my brain to think how we may bring her up to snuff."

Nell was aware that Emily wished only to assist, but this imparting of her situation to the earl mortified her. Again the color rose in her cheeks, and she said stiffly, "Please do not give it another thought, Mrs. Holmsly! I assure you that I am more than happy to merely observe the dancers. I have no wish to partake of such strenuous exercise."

"Pooh!" Emily retorted. "One would have to be dead not to wish to dance! It is the most delirious fun—passing gaily from hand to hand, and laughing and flirting. Oh, not for the world would I have you miss it!"

"But I must," Nell said firmly.

"Tonight, perhaps. But on the next occasion, you must be prepared to take your place in a set—with Hugh, and Lord Westwick, and Mr. Holmsly. Oh, indeed you must."

"I cannot think how I should learn to dance these intricate steps. Not from a library book, I assure you." Nell shook her head. "And I don't believe Aunt Longstreet has the intention of coming again, in any case."

"Not come again!" Emily looked horrified. She turned to Aunt Longstreet with the evident intention of cajoling the older woman into changing her mind. "Oh, ma'am, surely you must intend to come again. Why, no one stays in Bath who does not attend an assembly at least once a week!"

"Poppycock! My niece is not a spoiled girl who thinks of nothing but the elusive pleasures of society. Not for her, all these late nights and overcrowded rooms. She has a serious mind, not filled with fripperies and excitement. You would do well to take a page from her book," Aunt Longstreet admonished severely.

If Nell had been forced to respond in any way to this sally, she would have considered fainting dead away. Fortunately, she found herself no longer in her aunt's vicinity, but locked onto Lord Westwick's arm, with Sir Hugh flanking her other side. She blinked at first one and then the other of these two gentlemen, before saying humbly, "I thank you. Sometimes Aunt Longstreet is rather . . . outspoken. You don't think I should go back and rescue Mrs. Holmsly?"

"Emily is perfectly capable of fending for herself. And her husband is not given to allowing anyone to disparage her." Sir Hugh looked down (though only slightly) at his companion and added, "I beg you will forgive my sister, Miss Armstrong. She has an unfortunate habit of attempting to solve almost any problem which presents itself to her. And a great many of them, as you may note, are none of her business."

"Delightful creature, Mrs. Holmsly," Lord Westwick interjected. "She means to be your friend, I believe, Miss Armstrong. I trust you will bear that in mind, and not think too harshly of her."

"Of course not. I am very aware of her good intentions, but she had far better exercise them on someone more deserving!" Nell looked pleadingly at Sir Hugh. "My aunt does not appreciate having her will crossed, as I daresay you have noticed, sir. I fear she will make herself most unpleasant to your sister should Mrs. Holmsly appear to be at odds with her."

"If you think Miss Longstreet has it in her to reduce my sister to a quivering jelly, you do not know Emily," Sir Hugh teased. Then he added significantly, "And Emily has a husband and a brother to back her up."

Nell was very aware that she herself had no one to do likewise. But she was accustomed to her aunt's ways as few others could be. It all made for a challenging balancing act. Across the room Nell could see that the Holmslys continued to converse with Aunt Longstreet, whose vigorous cane-thumping could not be distinguished in such a noisy setting.

A tiny smile quivered at the corners of Nell's lips. "I doubt she will be caught at such a disadvantage another time," she remarked ruefully. Her aunt cast a glaring look about the room, and when her gaze lighted on Nell, she beckoned with an imperious hand. "I'd best return to her, if you wouldn't mind, Lord Westwick."

The earl paused and regarded her with concern. "If you're quite sure you wish to return . . ."

"Oh, yes. Else she'll become distressed. She is probably ready to leave now."

"Then, I shall accompany you home," Sir Hugh insisted.

"That would be very kind of you," Nell said. That disconcerting fluttery feeling lodged in her breast once more, much to her dismay. *You're five-and-twenty,* she chided herself. *Not nineteen. Behave accordingly.* Unfortunately, her inner self wasn't paying much attention, and her pulse remained quickened as she placed her hand on Sir Hugh's proffered arm.

Miss Longstreet did not wish for Sir Hugh's escort. She made herself quite plain about this, but the baronet paid her no heed. "Not only will you have my escort," he told her quietly but firmly, "but you will allow me to see you home in my carriage."

"I would rather have a sedan chair," she announced in piercing accents.

"But Miss Armstrong would prefer to be driven in my carriage," Sir Hugh announced without the least ground for his assertion, "and I have every intention of honoring her wish."

"Is that true?" Miss Longstreet demanded, glaring at Nell.

"Yes, indeed, Aunt Longstreet. For you know how difficult it was for us to maneuver into a sedan chair with our gowns, and how uncomfortable we were. I feel certain we will be much better accommodated in your godson's carriage."

"Humph," her aunt muttered.

Miss Longstreet at last seemed willing enough to leave the ballroom. She bid good-bye to the Holmslys, but ignored Lord Westwick, who stood aside to let the party pass. Nell extended her hand to the earl with a warm "Thank you!" Sir Hugh shepherded the ladies through the crowded room to the entrance hall. He had sent a servant to inform his driver that the carriage was wanted, but there had been insufficient time for it to arrive. Even after the ladies' pelisses had been claimed, the carriage had not appeared.

Fearing that his driver, having earlier been told that Sir Hugh would be two or three hours, had settled into some cozy inn for a brew, the baronet considered the possibility of hiring a hackney carriage. Fortune smiled on him, however, in the person of his friend Hopkins, who arrived in his carriage just as Hugh was considering the tongue-lashing he would receive from Miss Longstreet if he were to suggest a rented vehicle. He left his charges in the foyer and came out to meet his friend.

"Drat!" Hopkins exclaimed. "Knew I should have gotten here sooner. Don't tell me you're leaving already, old fellow."

"Hopkins, you are in the very nick of time. May I borrow your carriage?"

"My carriage?" His friend frowned, shaking his head. "But, Hugh, you have one of your own. Probably more than one. Yes, definitely more than one."

"But I need a carriage this instant in order to convey my godmother and her niece to their house in Queen Square. Why not come with us, and I will introduce you to them?"

Hopkins regarded him suspiciously. "This the old harridan from Westmorland?" he demanded.

"Mind your tongue! She's no more than six feet from here."

"Probably has ears as sharp as a dog's, too. You may take the carriage, but I'll not ride along, thank you." Hopkins was conveying these instructions to his coachman when Hugh brought the two ladies out into the light of the flambeaux on the areaway. He blinked in astonishment at their old-fashioned costumes, but gave a very creditable bow nonetheless. "Servant, ma'am," he said to Miss Longstreet. "Honored to offer you the use of my carriage."

Rosemarie Longstreet regarded it with a disparaging sniff. "Wouldn't have needed it if my godson had any control over his servants," she snapped as she allowed herself to be handed into the vehicle.

Coming directly behind, Hugh saw Nell give one of her charming, slightly apologetic smiles to Hopkins. Hugh said,

"Miss Armstrong, may I present my friend Horace Hopkins."

"How do you do?" Nell gave a little curtsy. "It was kind of you to accommodate us, Mr. Hopkins."

Hopkins, a rather short man, found himself looking up at the young woman. "Pray don't mention it," he insisted. "My pleasure."

After he had handed her into the carriage, he turned to Hugh and said in a low voice, "My word, she's the goddess Juno! You have the most remarkable relations, Hugh."

"I'm not related to either of them," Hugh reminded his friend, sotto voce.

"Those gowns . . ."

"Years out of fashion, I know, but I rather thought Miss Armstrong's suited her. Fanciful of me, perhaps."

His friend gave him an odd look but merely asked, "Shall I look for you back here in an hour?"

Sir Hugh shook his head. "I believe I'll call it a night. Thanks for your assistance, Hopkins." And so saying, he climbed into the carriage and closed the door behind him.

Chapter Six

Nell was intensely aware of the baronet sitting opposite them during the short ride to Queen Square. Since her aunt seemed lost in her own thoughts, Nell took it upon herself to converse with Sir Hugh. She mentioned that they had looked through the Peerage and found it wonderfully entertaining.

In the dim light that filtered through the carriage windows, Sir Hugh looked bemused. "Entertaining?"

"Well, yes, for Aunt Longstreet remembers some of these people from her come-out many years ago. It fascinates her to find what has become of them, who married who, and who had which children. Then she tells me stories of them from their youth—and decidedly amusing stories they are."

Sir Hugh regarded his godmother, still deep in her own thoughts, with something akin to disbelief. "Somehow I find it difficult to picture the two of you bent over the Peerage, doubled over with laughter."

Nell grinned, relieved to find herself relaxing in his company. "Well, they are seldom stories to anyone's credit, Sir Hugh, as you might imagine. But in light of the time that has passed, and the respectability of their current situations, we find the incongruity most delightful."

"Give me an example," he suggested.

"Ah, well, naming no names, but Aunt Longstreet told me of a certain peer of the realm, a viscount I believe he was, who had a penchant for ... um ... lifting small objects from the very best homes in London. This gentleman has been married three times, has nine children, and is a member of the present government!"

"Ah, I see what you mean. Do her stories shock you?"

"Oh, no. Eccentricity runs in my family, and I can only be comforted by finding that it is rampant even among the most wellborn."

Sir Hugh laughed. Nell warmed to the rich sound. He seemed genuinely delighted, the light in his eyes dancing with his enjoyment. How different a laugh could sound! One of the gentlemen at the Assembly Rooms that evening had brayed when he laughed, an exceedingly irritating sound. Especially as she was not at all certain that effete fellow hadn't been expressing his amusement at her costume. And Sir Hugh, after his first glance of astonishment, hadn't betrayed the slightest hint of criticism. Which further endeared him to her.

She had almost gotten up her courage to ask Sir Hugh about his sister's problematic intentions toward her, Nell, when the carriage drew up in front of the house in Queen Square. She waited while he handed Aunt Longstreet down onto the pavement. When he took her own hand, she was forced to grasp his firmly as she maneuvered the stiff bustled gown through the narrow doorway.

In her eagerness to find herself firmly on the ground, she slid slightly on the stair and the baronet's other hand came instantly to her waist to support her. His aid lasted only a moment, as she was soon safely on the ground. Oh, it was the smallest of actions, but Nell chose to tuck it, along with the sensation it aroused in her, away in her mind. It was the sort of detail one needed to embellish a daydream, and she might have great need of daydreams when they returned to Longstreet Manor.

* * *

Nell was convinced that Aunt Longstreet had some devilry afoot. It was not so much that her mood was low; in fact, if anything there seemed to be a suppressed excitement about her. The day after the assembly, Nell happened upon Rosemarie in the study with a volume of the Peerage open. When the older woman heard her niece enter the room, she quickly snapped shut the book she had been perusing and slid it away.

"Can I help you find something?" Nell asked cautiously.

"Nothing! I was just paging through in the hopes of coming upon a familiar name."

Though Nell did not believe this for a minute, she merely nodded. Since the two women had gone straight to bed the previous evening, Nell now asked, "Did you enjoy yourself last night, Aunt Longstreet?"

Rosemarie Longstreet scowled, but said in only a slightly disparaging tone, "What is there to enjoy in such a crush of people? It was hot and the wine was watered, just as one would expect. I trust you do not cherish the ambition to attend any more assemblies."

"Oh, I don't know. There was such a festive air to it," Nell said dreamily. "The ladies looked so pretty in their finery— and the gentlemen so handsome. I thought Mrs. Holmsly's husband particularly fascinating."

Her aunt eyed her speculatively. "Seemed a dull dog to me. Talked of nothing but the condition of the roads."

"I saw them dancing as we were waiting for the carriage. They make such a fine-looking couple." Nell paused, drawing her hand absently across a volume of the Peerage. "Aunt Longstreet, does your dislike of Lord Westwick have its root in the past?"

Her aunt's face took on a fierce, determined look. "That is none of your business, missy. You are not to be making friends with him, either, do you hear? I was most displeased to see you stroll off on his arm, let me tell you."

"Unless you can give me a reason for being anything but pleasant to the man, I shall have to decide for myself, ma'am."

"Don't be impertinent!" Rosemarie snapped. "If I tell you he is to be shunned, you must accept my word."

"My dear aunt, there are so few people of whom you approve that I would be without any acquaintance if I followed your strictures!"

"This is quite different."

"In what way?"

Rosemarie pursed her lips stubbornly. "You don't need to know."

Nell turned away. "Very well. Shall I bring you a cup of tea now, Aunt?"

"Yes." And though she rarely said it, she added, "Thank you, Helen."

Sir Hugh discovered, when he waited on his sister the following day, that she was at work again hatching plans.

"I inquired last evening, after your Queen Square ladies left, if any of the matrons present had hired a dancing instructor for her children." Emily's eyes twinkled. "People are always so ready to tell you these things. I think it has something to do with their delight in talking about their own children. Remind me not to constantly rattle on about Walter when he is older."

"You feel it is acceptable to 'rattle on' about him now, do you, Emily?"

She laughed. "Of course I do. He's only a baby. But when he is—oh—ten or eleven, and has acquired some real skills beyond smiling, I shall be forced to button my lips about him, for I refuse to embarrass him by telling the world at large what an elegant dancer he is, or how well he rides a horse."

"Well, perhaps he won't be an elegant dancer, or ride a horse well," Hugh consoled her.

"Fustian! Of course he will," she assured him. "With his father and you as examples, I do not see how he can possibly manage to do otherwise."

"And yet, some of us are grave disappointments to our parents."

"Walter shan't be. Anyhow, that is beside the point, Hugh, and I wish you would not distract me this way."

"Beg pardon."

"Now, Mrs. Gorton was the most helpful of the ladies with whom I spoke. She has two daughters and three sons, all of an age to be instructed by a dancing master, though the youngest is under ten, I believe."

"And tell me, Emily, why you have developed this intense interest in dancing masters," he suggested.

"But, Hugh, it is obvious! Miss Armstrong needs one, but that dragon to whom she is companion is scarcely likely to hire one for her."

"No, she most certainly is not. And I trust you don't plan to do so, either."

"Well, I don't. But I have hit upon the perfect scheme, nevertheless."

Sir Hugh sighed and shook his head. "Emily, you are way beyond your depth here, my girl. I fancy this all has to do, ultimately, with your master plan to rescue my inheritance. Pray abandon your efforts on my behalf. Miss Longstreet will decide how to dispose of her property without consulting either of us, and I fear any efforts on your part will serve only to irritate her already overburdened nerves. I trust you noticed that she gave poor Lord Westwick a direct cut last evening. So much for your initial moves on my account."

A tiny frown creased Emily's brow. "That was most unfortunate. But you must know, Hugh, that my efforts on Miss Armstrong's behalf are not entirely because of you. I feel for the dear girl, living with that ogre. She deserves better, and I intend to see that she gets it."

"Emily, you scarcely know her! She may be perfectly content with her lot in life."

"Surely you jest! No one could be content to spend her entire life caring for that cantankerous relation. It is the worst sort of servitude."

Hugh made an impatient gesture. "My dear sister, not everyone has the advantages that you and I do. You cannot be so naive as to think you can right all the ills of society because they distress you! Miss Armstrong is a young woman who strikes me as capable of making the best of her position and not allowing herself to be cowed by my godmother. Anything you try to do for her is more likely to cause her grief than to make her life more comfortable."

"I cannot agree," his sister retorted. "And, besides, Hugh, what harm could it do her to learn some country-dances with the Gorton children?"

"Is that what you have in mind?" Hugh ran an agitated hand through his thick brown hair, managing to disorder it considerably. "Emily, she's twenty-odd years old. She would feel foolish dancing with children, to say nothing of the fact that she doesn't at this moment even know of the existence of the Gortons."

"What has that to say to anything? She didn't know me a week ago, either. And I shall accompany her to the Gortons, and play the pianoforte, so she needn't feel the least out of place."

Hugh stared at his sister. "You will play the pianoforte? Emily, have you lost your mind? You scarcely know the Gortons, and, though I trust you know several country tunes, you couldn't possibly wish to perform them for a group of children not out of the schoolroom."

Emily flushed. "Perhaps not. I daresay they have a governess who would serve better than I. But I shall accompany

Nell there, and perhaps even take part in the dancing, if they need another female. Don't you remember what fun those dancing parties were when we were young, Hugh? Mrs. Gorton said she invites a number of young people to join her own children, enough to make up a decent set. It is the only way Miss Armstrong will learn."

"Emily, you don't even know if Miss Armstrong wishes to learn."

Emily's chin lifted perceptibly. "I shall ask her. And I beg you won't interfere, Hugh. Allow me to at least offer her the opportunity."

"Very well. But you will be well served if she dismisses you as a meddlesome busybody!"

It would not have occurred to Nell to dismiss anyone as charming as Emily Holmsly as a "meddlesome busybody," but she was astonished by her guest's suggestion. "Oh, I am certain I am a great deal too old to learn to dance," she insisted, her face and voice earnest. "How kind of you to think of such a scheme, though. You have been a great deal too good to me."

"Pooh! Not a bit of it. And no one is ever too old to learn to dance, Nell, I promise you."

Emily had asked to see Nell alone after the briefest of greetings to Rosemarie, and Nell could only be glad that her aunt hadn't overheard the plan. She wouldn't have hesitated to call Emily a meddlesome busybody! But Nell was shaking her head, very aware that such a plan could not possibly succeed.

"Even if I could learn, there would really be very little purpose," Nell explained. "After all, we shall only be in Bath for a short stay, and Aunt Longstreet has already declared her intention not to attend any more assemblies."

"And so she needn't!" Emily grinned conspiratorially at her companion. "Much better that she stay home, if she takes no pleasure in them. But you! I saw how your eyes glittered with excitement. And I may as well tell you that it is a delight to meet someone who finds them new and promising, for you are like a girl just come-out, except that you are a great deal more mature. And if you knew how to execute the country-dances, you could go to the local assemblies in Westmorland."

"I'm afraid that isn't likely. That is about the last thing on earth that my aunt would countenance, and there is really no purpose in it."

"No purpose! But, my dear girl, how are you to meet eligible men?"

Nell's eyes danced. "Ah, I see what it is. You are intent on seeing me married. You must understand, Emily, that I have no thought of marrying."

Her visitor looked horrified. "No thought of marrying! Surely that cannot be so. Why, every woman wishes to marry and have a family and settle into a home of her own."

"Nonetheless, my intention is to remain with Aunt Longstreet and make my home at Longstreet Manor."

"But your aunt won't live forever," Emily protested. "And then what will become of you?"

"I trust Aunt Longstreet will provide an independence for me in her will." Nell lifted her shoulders in a helpless shrug. "If she doesn't, well, I can seek a position as companion when the time comes. I will no doubt have a great deal of experience by then."

"Entirely too much," Emily muttered. She appeared to be on the point of expostulating with Nell when the butler Woodbridge appeared in the doorway to announce, "Mr. Bentley has called, miss, and wishes to know if you are at home."

Nell felt somewhat surprised at receiving a visit from the librarian, and wondered briefly if Emily might misinterpret his calling in Queen Square. Nonetheless, she did not feel that she could turn him away. "Please show him in, Woodbridge." And turning to Emily she explained, "Mr. Bentley is a librarian who has been looking out for some books for me and my aunt. You may have encountered him at the lending library."

As she had feared, Emily's eyes lit with suspicion. "I daresay I may have, but no librarian has ever come to my home."

Mr. Bentley looked a little disconcerted to find that Nell was entertaining company, and he immediately exclaimed, "I beg your pardon for interrupting, Miss Armstrong! Your butler failed to mention that you had a visitor."

"You are very welcome," Nell assured him. "This is Mrs. Holmsly, my aunt's godson's sister. Emily, this is Mr. Bentley."

The young man bowed punctiliously, awkwardly shifting the large pile of books he carried. "A pleasure, ma'am." When he turned to Nell, he added, "If you would prefer my coming another time . . ."

"No, please. Have a seat and show us what you've brought."

Mr. Bentley's awkwardness vanished when he started to discuss the various volumes he carried with him. Emily became a mere observer as Nell questioned the young man on the authors and the content of the books. He had a wealth of interesting information at his fingertips, and was more than willing to share it.

"This one," he said, holding up a sizable book in half leather, "is a guidebook to Bath, but it covers more than the usual sights. Bath's hidden treasures are to be found in here, and a history of the city that goes back far beyond the Aquae Solis of the Romans. There is an account of Solsbury Hill and the myth of Bladud and his swine." He smiled engagingly. "And you will enjoy the influence the goddess Minerva has had on the town."

"I shall most certainly read it with care," Nell promised.

"This history I brought especially for your aunt, because it discusses the influence of the latter half of the last century on the changes happening today."

Nell nodded. "Yes, indeed. That should please her—provided the influence is considered an important one."

"Oh, yes. It's written by a rather curmudgeonly old fellow," Mr. Bentley admitted, with just the tiniest smile. "But he is considered quite an authority, mind."

"Perfect. I daresay it would bore me to flinders?"

"No, no. But the style is rather more florid than our contemporary ear is accustomed to. You would probably find yourself skimming through the more prosaic passages."

Nell felt certain she had been right in the first instance, that the book would be oppressively boring to her. But she had noticed that when someone took an interest in you—and she had to admit to herself that perhaps Mr. Bentley had—they had a tendency to believe you shared the same tastes and even the same level of intelligence that they did. This could be disconcerting, especially in the case of a man like Mr. Bentley, who was undoubtedly extremely well read.

Though Rosemarie frequently insisted that Nell was of a serious turn of mind, Nell herself was not so sure. True, she did not indulge in frivolous activities, or even in particularly amusing reading, but that was more, she suspected, for lack of opportunity than real intent. The library at Longstreet Manor ran to dull histories and uplifting essays. Aunt Longstreet did not subscribe to any of the more popular journals of fashion—thus their embarrassment of the previous evening.

Mr. Bentley had brought one novel with him, and he placed it tentatively in Nell's hands. "This may be of no interest to you," he disclaimed, "but many of the ladies who frequent the lending library have assured me it is not the usual farrago of nonsense. I will take it back if you should disapprove of such reading, of course."

"*Mansfield Park*, by A Lady," Nell read. "Do you know the story, Mr. Bentley?"

"I have not myself read it as yet, but I understand that it is about a modest young woman coming to live with her more prosperous, and perhaps less upright, relations."

Emily, who had not spoken until now, giggled. "How splendid! If you have no interest in reading it, Nell, I shall certainly take it home with me!"

"I think I should read at least the first chapter or two to see for myself whether or not I like it," Nell said. "Not many novels have come in my way."

"Poor child!" Emily consoled her. "Those novels Mr. Bentley apostrophizes as a 'farrago of nonsense' have whiled away many a dull hour for me."

Nell thought Mr. Bentley's smile was just a shade complaisant. "Oh, yes, many of the ladies who patronize the library are quite taken with *The Mysteries of Udolpho* and the like. These are highly adventurous and exciting stories, no doubt, but haven't a wisp of credulity to them. While *Mansfield Park* I believe is quite a different story. My understanding is that the author satirizes certain social pretentions while exhibiting the virtue of her heroine."

"Oh, well, then, I probably shouldn't care for it," Emily protested with a moue of disappointment.

Nell laughed at her new friend's outrageous observation, but Mr. Bentley seemed to take her seriously. "Oh, I feel certain you would, Mrs. Holmsly!" he said, his brow contracting. "I am told the writing is especially fine."

"No doubt, no doubt," Emily agreed. She gave a little tug to the paisley shawl she wore. "I shall await Miss Armstrong's opinion of the book before I consider reading it."

Mr. Bentley turned to his hostess. "Will you try it then, ma'am? I brought it especially for you, as I had no reason to believe your aunt would be interested in a contemporary novel."

"Certainly, Mr. Bentley. You were kind to think of us, and especially generous to come here with the books. I would have come to the library very soon, I assure you!"

"Well, it had been several days since you were there, and, as you can see, I had accumulated quite a stack of books for you to consider." He seemed to hesitate before he spoke again, more diffidently. "I thought perhaps I could call again in a few days, to see if you wished me to take back any of the volumes."

"How kind of you, but, you know, I am perfectly capable of bringing the books to the library myself." Nell smiled to take any sting from this rejoinder. "I mustn't expect such service in future."

Once again Emily thrust herself into the conversation, this time to say, "Yes, my dear Nell, but at the library it is always so busy, and the patrons expect such a hushed atmosphere. You and Mr. Bentley would not be able to discuss what you had read. And I think Mr. Bentley would be most interested in your opinion of some of these books, especially the novel."

"Indeed I should!" Mr. Bentley agreed, bestowing a grateful smile on Mrs. Holmsly. "But of course I would not come if you should not like it, Miss Armstrong!"

"It is a great deal too good of you," Nell temporized. "But no doubt my aunt would like the opportunity to thank you in person for your kindness to us both."

Mr. Bentley looked as though this prospect would not provide him with much of a treat, but he stoutly proclaimed that he would come again. Then he rose to take his departure, making a polite bow to Mrs. Holmsly and clasping Nell's hand briefly but firmly. When he had left the room, Emily shook her head and said, "That is no way to encourage a suitor, Nell—threatening him with your aunt!"

"Mr. Bentley is not a suitor, Emily," Nell informed her with a frown. "And I do not at all wish to encourage him."

"Whyever not? He seems a decent enough fellow."

"I feel certain that he is, which is reason enough not to lead him astray."

"Lead him astray? How could you possibly lead him astray?" Emily asked, astonished.

"It would be dishonest in me to allow him to spend time with me, believing we could develop a liking for one another. As I mentioned earlier, I have no intention of marrying."

Emily shook her head, refusing to accept this pronouncement. "But, Nell, you must marry."

"Oh, no. Not every woman was meant to marry, my dear Emily. Look at Aunt Longstreet."

"You are not the least like your aunt, Nell. Marriage would be the perfect solution for you."

Nell was not willing to argue the point with her new friend, so she said, "We shall see." But she knew very well that decision had long since been made.

Chapter Seven

S ir Hugh had no intention of visiting the ladies in Queen Square on the day following the assembly. For one thing, he was convinced that his sister would go there to propose her idea of the dancing instruction, and he did not wish Miss Armstrong to think that he had anything to do with that proposal. For another, he was not in the mood to endure his godmother's sharp tongue. True, she had been distracted the previous evening and consequently had not managed to say anything particularly devastating on the drive home, but he had no dependence on her distracted mood lasting for more than a short while.

So he would not have come near Queen Square if he had not happened to encounter his sister in Milsom Street. And he was not at all surprised to hear that Miss Armstrong had politely rejected Emily's offer of the dancing lessons. He had expected no less. What he had not expected was Emily's account of the librarian's visit.

"One can tell he has a *tendre* for her," Emily insisted. "Why else would he be bringing books to that household? Certainly not to please your godmother! And he looks at her in just such a way . . ."

"At my godmother?" Hugh asked, laughing.

"No, gudgeon, at Nell." Emily sighed at the romanticism of it. "Do you suppose librarians make enough to support wives?"

"I'm afraid I haven't the first idea," he admitted.

"Of course, there would be no difficulty if your god-mother were to give her a bride portion, but I fear Miss Longstreet is not to be trusted to do any such thing."

"My dear Emily, your thoughts as usual have far out-stripped the events to which they relate. This poor fellow did no more than bring some books to the ladies, and already you have him married but for the want of a bride portion."

Emily wrinkled her nose in deep thought. "Do you suppose he suspects her to be an heiress, Hugh? Do you think that perhaps he is merely ingratiating himself with the two ladies so that he can marry Nell and inherit all Miss Longstreet's property?"

"I shouldn't think so," he said, shaking his head with frustration. "Emily, my advice to you is to go home and manage your own household instead of attempting to manage the lives of three people you scarcely know."

"You would not be so cavalier if you had been there and seen Mr. Bentley's obvious intention," his sister replied haughtily. "Remember that Nell is not accustomed to the attentions of young and attractive men out there in the wilds of Westmorland. She could easily be swayed by a kind word and a thoughtful gesture."

"She did not appear to me to be a young woman so easily influenced. In fact, my impression was that Miss Armstrong is of excellent understanding and strong will. She would have to be to scrape along with her aunt. You are quite out if you think she has a fluffy head on her shoulders."

"Oh, intelligence and will have nothing to do with love!" Emily declared passionately. "Surely you know that, Hugh. If Nell were to fall in love with Mr. Bentley, all her intelligence would be as nothing. And her will! Why, she would use it to achieve the end of becoming his wife, I daresay."

The picture Emily painted was not at all pleasing to Hugh. Though he realized that his sister was weaving a fantasy that had almost no grounding in reality, he could not help but wonder if the seed that had been sown by Mr. Bentley's visit in Queen Square might not indeed take root. He concealed his displeasure with difficulty as he took his leave of his sister. Why did he feel so bothered? For honor's sake, he hoped that it was not concern about his inheritance. And yet, what other reason had he to feel what amounted to a real stab of alarm?

Perhaps, he thought, as he strode off in the direction of Queen Square, it was because his own evaluation of Miss Armstrong did not ignore the fact that she was a babe in the woods where the world was concerned. In that, certainly, Emily was correct. Miss Armstrong might easily be overwhelmed by the admiration of a young man who had nothing to recommend him except a pleasant face and a gracious manner. If nothing else, was it not Sir Hugh's duty in some measure to keep an eye on her and prevent her from enacting any sort of folly? Surely he owed that much to his godmother, who could not be expected to be any more up to snuff than her niece where the social world of Bath was concerned. His brow cleared as this logical reasoning made his concern fully explainable.

Rosemarie was not disposed to look favorably on Sir Hugh's visit. "We saw you only last night," she protested. "What are you doing here this afternoon?"

"Heaven knows," he murmured, giving Nell a rueful glance. "It is customary, in Bath, to pay a call on the ladies you have recently escorted, to inquire as to their comfort after the rigors of attending a social function."

"Horsefeathers! As if Helen and I weren't stout enough to make the smallest excursion. If I were that decrepit, I would not have come to Bath in the first place."

"So you were out first thing this morning taking the waters at the Pump Room, were you?" Hugh asked.

His godmother glared at him. "We don't take the waters every day. They are far too disgusting to drink all that often. I suspect that they would poison you if you drank them every day."

"Do you?" Hugh's brows rose. "I don't believe I've heard of anyone being poisoned by them. Have you?"

When Rosemarie only snorted, her niece met his interested gaze with merry eyes. They were remarkably pretty eyes, he noted. And her complexion was so fair that her feelings easily showed in the quick rise and fall of color in softly rounded cheeks. Her lips curved delightfully with those tucked-away smiles she half concealed so well. Bemused, he realized she was speaking to him.

"You can never be too careful, Sir Hugh. Aunt Longstreet has taken note of all the invalids who congregate at the Pump Room, and it is her opinion that any number of them may as easily be harmed as helped by the waters, since very few of them appear to be cured when they leave Bath."

"Ah, I see. I have not myself indulged in the waters on a regular basis, but I have to admit that they taste vile. Still, some people do swear by them. Have you considered bathing in them?"

His godmother narrowed her eyes. "And just what would be the point of that? Are you hoping I'll drown myself?"

"I'm quite certain no one has ever drowned in the baths, ma'am," he assured her. "Apparently the minerals in the water, and its warmth, are particularly good for the gout."

"And you would be an authority on gout, would you, young man?"

"My father had it, so I do have some experience at second hand."

Miss Armstrong, rather than her aunt, showed a decided interest. "And he found the baths helpful?"

"On many occasions. Of course, some people say it is all in one's head, the benefits of such a treatment. That if you expect some comfort, you will convince yourself that you have received it."

"Fools," muttered his godmother. "I've seen it happen myself."

Miss Armstrong's brow knit in thought. "Well, Aunt, I'm not sure that it matters, so long as one perceives a benefit. On the other hand, perhaps if one is convinced that no benefit will be achieved, one denies oneself the chance of getting one."

The older woman locked eyes with her niece. Hugh, delighted with Nell's response, thought there was a battle of wills silently occurring between the two even as he watched. Miss Longstreet glared her intimidating scowl, and her niece regarded her with another of those tucked-away smiles. After a very long pause, Miss Longstreet looked away and said, "Perhaps one day I would be willing to try the baths, but only if you were to accompany me into the water, Helen. And I have no intention of paying a fortune, mind!"

"Certainly not, aunt," her niece said with deceptive meekness.

Sir Hugh would have offered his services in escorting them, except that he was aware his godmother would take the opportunity to give him a proper set-down. Instead he asked, "Are there any evening entertainments to which I might escort you ladies? Or might I procure tickets for a musical evening later in the week?"

"What sort of musical evening?" Rosemarie demanded suspiciously. "No, no, don't tell me. You may tell Helen. She's the musical one. If she should like it, you may get the tickets. Now, go away, both of you. I need my nap."

Saying this, she laid her head back against the chair and closed her eyes. Miss Armstrong placed a blanket over her aunt's knees and beckoned Sir Hugh through a door into the smaller parlor. Sir Hugh saw a number of books lying on the table there and assumed these were the books the librarian had brought.

He picked up one of the volumes and turned it over, recognizing a popular guidebook to Bath. "My sister mentioned that the young man at the lending library had brought by some books for you and your aunt. That was exceptionally kind of him, especially considering the treatment to which my godmother subjected him on the occasion I happened upon the two of you. Or perhaps it was not the same man?" he asked blandly.

"Yes, it was Mr. Bentley, the same young man. Aunt Longstreet has managed to be abrupt with him on more than one occasion, but he is so good as to overlook her ill humor."

"Very good of him indeed. And yet, I cannot help but wonder if his advent at your home was not something of a surprise?" He made it sound a question, but Nell did no more than blink at him. "What I mean is, unless you had suggested that he call here, perhaps you did not welcome his intrusion. My godmother might consider it something of a liberty."

"I did not suggest that he come, Sir Hugh, but I did not find it distressing that he did. My aunt is not as yet aware that he called, as she was resting at the time. All things considered, I believe I shan't tell her that he did."

Hugh felt suspicion prod at him. "And why is that?"

Miss Armstrong—Nell; as his sister would call her—moved to the small sofa, straightened a pillow, then went to the window and lightly touched the curtain. "It is my policy not to distress my aunt any more than is strictly necessary, Sir Hugh. If I felt that there was something improper about Mr. Bentley's visit, or that he had some nefarious purpose in discovering where we lived, then I should certainly inform my aunt. But I have no such suspicion." She turned then and regarded him curiously. "Have you?"

"No. I merely find the behavior a trifle—odd." Sir Hugh could hear the stiffness in his own voice.

"Your sister didn't."

"My sister is a romantic."

"And you are not."

Sir Hugh did not like the flat way she said it, as though it were not to his credit. "I am a practical man, Miss Armstrong. Sometimes I ask myself what motive a man has for doing what he does. That may not be a very trusting attitude, but it is a prudent one. I assure you that I do not suspect Mr. Bentley of any unworthy purpose. No doubt he is precisely the generous fellow he presents himself as. But because his actions are somewhat out of the ordinary, and because they circumspectly touch my godmother, I choose not to overlook them. I hope you won't take my interest amiss."

"Not at all. But I trust you have no intention of quizzing poor Mr. Bentley on his kindly impulse to befriend my aunt and myself."

"I intend to do nothing but discover the young man's character, by having a word with his employer or someone who knows him."

A flush brightened Nell's cheeks, and she frowned. "You could lose him his job, Sir Hugh. What if his employer thought it unacceptable that he brought us books? I must ask that you not risk such a resolution."

"My dear Miss Armstrong, that is hardly likely to happen. I would of course be circumspect."

But she had come to a halt in front of him, the frown still creasing her brow. "I cannot feel sanguine about your plan, and I should hate to be responsible for something untoward happening. Rather, I would tell him not to come here again. Would that meet with your approval?"

Feeling that somehow matters had gotten out of hand, Hugh abandoned his stiff tone and said, "It will not be necessary for you to tell him not to come again, Miss Armstrong! I beg your pardon for raising the issue in the first place. I had no intention of distressing you. If you are confident of Mr. Bentley's goodwill, I shall pursue the matter no further."

"Thank you." Nell's high color ebbed, and she smiled a little wryly at him. "You know, there is no chance of his imposing on us, Sir Hugh. When you consider my aunt's disposition, you must realize that at the first hint of anything untoward, she would be likely to dispose of him in a fearsome manner."

"True," he agreed, amazed and grateful she hadn't taken offense. "I could find it in me to pity him, if she did. But enough of Mr. Bentley. Tell me what my godmother meant that you were the one who appreciated music."

They had been standing all this time, but now she waved him to a chair and took one opposite. "Aunt Longstreet finds music soporific, I fear. I have only to sit down at the pianoforte for her to fall asleep. I, on the other hand, find music invigorating. I am not a particularly accomplished player, but I thoroughly enjoy it."

"And would you welcome attending a musical evening here in Bath?"

When she laughed, the sound was deliciously rippling, rich and melodious. "Oh, yes, I should enjoy it of all things. But I am inclined to believe that Aunt Longstreet would be dreadfully bored. In all likelihood she would fall into a slumber and snore!"

"Does she do that often in the country?"

"Most of our neighbors know better than to invite her for anything of a musical nature. She is not in the habit of going about much—at home. I was quite surprised to learn of her intention to come to Bath."

"Yes, you may imagine my astonishment in encountering her at the circulating library. I had not the first notion that she was in the city."

Nell shook her head slowly, a worried frown drawing her brows together. "I have actually been a little concerned about that, Sir Hugh. I'd thought of seeking your advice . . ."

"By all means! What is it that troubles you?"

For a moment the young woman didn't speak. He watched her expressive countenance as she continued to hesitate. He endeavored to look trustworthy, and was rewarded when she nodded slightly. Then she said, "Where to begin? I suppose when Mrs. Dorsey's letter arrived. Before that Aunt Longstreet had never in all the time I'd been with her suggested the possibility of traveling so far as one of the lakes. In fact, she had impressed upon me her truly deep dislike of travel."

"She has mentioned as much to me, as well."

"Yes, and yet after reading Mrs. Dorsey's letter, she turned to me, with quite a wicked look on her face, and said, 'Helen, we shall go to Bath.' I have seldom been so astonished in my life."

"Do you know what the contents of the letter were?"

Nell shook her head. "Not really. Aunt Longstreet indicated that Mrs. Dorsey recommended the Bath waters for her gout, but I hardly think that is possible."

Sir Hugh's brows rose. "Why not?"

"Because she and Mrs. Dorsey have corresponded for many years, and the subject has never been broached before. Why should she do so now?"

"Perhaps Miss Longstreet had only recently mentioned her gout to her friend."

"Aunt Longstreet has never mentioned it at all! She likes her friends to believe that she is in perfect health for a woman of her age—to make them all envious, I believe." She smiled at him, and added, "She is given to describing her constitution as robust."

"In some ways, I should think it is."

"Oh, yes. But, Sir Hugh, since we have come to Bath, she

has not contacted Mrs. Dorsey at all, and I am informed that the good lady lives but a few blocks from here."

"It is easy enough to imagine a falling out between them," he suggested, bearing in mind his aunt's temperament.

"Possibly." But Nell sounded skeptical. "Aunt Longstreet wrote back to her that time, however, and has since had a letter from her, which I believe she may also have answered. But I don't think she could have mentioned that we were coming to Bath!"

"Odd, certainly. What do you know of Mrs. Dorsey?"

"Very little, except that they have known each other forever. I had hoped you might recognize the name, as I understand you are a regular visitor to Bath."

"I am, yes, but I cannot recall a Mrs. Dorsey. I did know a Ralph Dorsey a few years ago, but I believe he no longer lives here. In fact, I think he took orders and is serving in a parish not far from London."

"I suppose she might be his mother," Nell said uncertainly. "Did you know where he lived?"

"In the lower part of town, I believe, but that is merely a guess." Sir Hugh regarded her curiously. "What is it you feel is amiss, Miss Armstrong?"

Nell made an all-encompassing gesture. "Everything. I know that sounds dramatic, but consider. Aunt Longstreet never leaves home, unless she has a very pressing reason. She never spends money if she can avoid it. And yet here we are in Bath—Bath, of all places. Why, it is almost as expensive to rent a place here as in the metropolis, I daresay. And then she told me we were coming at Mrs. Dorsey's suggestion, but we have made no attempt to contact Mrs. Dorsey. When I asked my aunt why her friend had not yet called upon us, she said, 'She's probably out of town.'"

"It's possible," he suggested.

"But not very likely, is it, after her recommending that we

ome. Oh, no, I think Mrs. Dorsey is in Bath, but she does
ot know that we are here."

"What possible reason could Miss Longstreet have for not
ontacting her?"

"I ask myself that daily," Nell admitted, "but I have ar-
ived at no reasonable answer. And then there is the matter of
Lord Westwick."

"Lord Westwick?"

"Yes, he came to visit us, and my aunt turned him away.
When I reproached her with that, she was positively gleeful.
She said, 'We are making progress, Helen.' But she would
not enlighten me on her meaning. This morning she insisted
I should shun his lordship but would give me no explanation.
Do you not think that odd?"

"For my godmother, no. She appears to dislike a great
many people." Including myself, he might have added.

"Well, yes, but this is different, I think. It's difficult for me
to put my finger on the problem, but when you take it in con-
junction with her strange behavior with regard to Mrs.
Dorsey, I cannot help but be concerned that there is mischief
afoot."

Sir Hugh did not bother to ask her what type of mischief
she suspected, because it was clear that Nell was at a loss on
that score. Instead he asked, "In what way do you think I
might be of service, Miss Armstrong? I should be happy to
assist in any way I can."

She smiled gratefully. "I believe there is something, if you
would be so kind. It is not just a matter of curiosity with me,
you understand. I am not a naturally suspicious or even particularly curious person, in the ordinary way. If you were to
put out inquiries about a Mrs. Dorsey, a Gertrude Dorsey, I
would be most appreciative. For if I knew her direction, I
could pay her a visit and attempt to sort this matter out."

"You would call on her without your aunt's knowledge?"

Nell raised her chin. "I would. Do you think that repre hensible of me?"

"Not at all." His lips twisted ruefully. "But if she should find out about it, she would not be pleased. In fact, she might very well do something drastic—like turn you off. And I canno think that would be an acceptable conclusion to the affair."

Nell frowned but eventually shook her head. "I don't think she would turn me off. I should certainly be in her black books for a while, but I am not exactly an employee Longstreet Manor is my home, for as long as Aunt Longstreet lives. That is understood."

Sir Hugh wondered by whom it was understood. He could not feel as certain as Nell that Miss Longstreet would not cast her out if she did something so counter to her will as to truly irritate that old autocrat. But he decided it was not his place to correct her at this point. He could, he felt certain, take the blame should anything go amiss. So he said only, "I shall see what I can do about discovering Mrs. Dorsey's address. In the meantime, I should like to take you and my godmother to a concert of Italian music this Friday evening, if that would suit you. Your aunt did say that it was your decision to make."

"Oh, that would be delightful!" Nell beamed at him. "And I will do my best to see that my aunt does not fall asleep and disgrace herself."

"Excellent. Until Friday, then, when I will let you know the results of my inquiries." He rose and bowed to her, taking the opportunity to observe her more closely. She was not, as his friend Hopkins had suggested the previous evening, the goddess Juno. Though tall, she was actually a little on the delicate side, with thin wrists and a tiny waist, and feet no wider than a child's. But there was so much strength and determination in her face, and forthright honesty in her eyes, that one might well judge her at first sight to resemble that Roman divinity.

Sir Hugh was accustomed to beauties who hadn't a thought in their heads, or bluestockings who had serious and weighty thoughts in theirs. Where did one place Miss Armstrong among this female acquaintance? She was not, certainly, of a nature similar to Emily's. He could not imagine her doing the impulsive things his sister did. And yet he could not quite believe she was the studious, disdaining woman his godmother chose to portray. There was something elusive about Nell. She would no doubt have laughed at the idea of anyone considering her mysterious, but Sir Hugh did feel there was a great deal more to her and her situation than met the eye.

What disturbed Sir Hugh as he left her in the smaller parlor of the Queen Square house, was that she might indeed be swayed by the librarian's attentions. Not that he knew anything against Mr. Bentley. The fellow seemed worthy enough, and Hugh suspected that he was from a good family as well. Also, one could scarcely complain of his mediocre prospects when Nell herself insisted that she had none. But Hugh wished he hadn't given his promise that he wouldn't investigate the librarian. In his mind Mr. Bentley was a far more promising subject for investigation than was Mrs. Dorsey.

And what was it Nell suspected her aunt had in mind? There was undoubtedly a logical explanation for why she hadn't gotten in touch with her old friend and correspondent. Hugh paused at the corner of Barton Street, a frown creasing his brow. If Nell took the matter seriously, it behooved him to do likewise, he supposed. His godmother might very well be intent on making trouble, and Hugh could foresee himself being the person called upon to calm whatever storm she set in motion. Knowing his godmother as he did, Hugh did not doubt that she was capable of causing a great deal of damage—if she had a mind to.

Nell had indicated that Lord Westwick figured rather

prominently in his godmother's designs. And in no good fashion, either. Miss Longstreet had given his lordship the cut direct the previous evening at the assembly, despite the fact that the two were acquainted many years ago.

Sir Hugh tipped his hat to a passing acquaintance, but continued walking. His thoughts were focused on trying to recall what he knew of the earl's history. He and Lord Westwick were by no means close, nor had the earl and Hugh's father been on more than nodding terms. Some bad blood there? Hugh could not remember any talk of trouble. His father had never hinted at any family disagreement with Westwick or given any indication of a personal dislike. They had merely seemed to keep a certain distance, the kind of distance one kept when one had few interests in common or one seldom encountered the other. Both of which were likely in this case.

Sir Hugh believed that the earl and countess had lived the greater part of their time in Bath, rather than on their estate in Westmorland. Lord Westwick rode and hunted and maintained an admirable stable, even in town, as well as owning a horse farm not far from Bath. This last, in fact, had apparently taken the place of his estate in his affections, though his lady was not deemed to have shared his enthusiasm for horses or even for the horse farm. She had remained largely in their house in Bath, a splendid home overlooking luxurious parkland and the River Avon.

The clatter of wheels from a passing hackney recalled Hugh to his surroundings, and he realized his steps had brought him to Parade Street, not far from where Lord Westwick lived. On an impulse, he made his way there, climbed to the front door, and plied the brass knocker. It was only a moment before a footman answered the door and assured Sir Hugh that his master was at home. Hugh was shown into a pleasant, sunny room elegantly furnished with divans and chairs covered in burgundy brocade, trimmed with gold tassels. It was an enchanting, whimsical room, with dancing rainbows made by a forest of crystals hung in the windows.

A voice spoke behind him. "This is indeed a pleasant surprise. How kind of you to call, Sir Hugh."

The baronet turned to see his host standing in the doorway, a warm smile on his patrician face. Hugh thought the earl looked a little peaked, as though he had perhaps not had a restful night, but that might have been his fancy. "Lord Westwick. I beg you will forgive my intrusion, but I find I cannot be easy about my godmother's treatment of you at the assembly last night."

Lord Westwick waved him to a seat and offered a glass of sherry. When the baronet refused, he seated himself in the opposite chair. His expression, however, was not particularly encouraging. "You are not responsible for your godmother's actions, Sir Hugh. Rosemarie was a willful girl, and I suspect she has become something of a tyrant as she grows older. I do not envy Miss Armstrong her position as companion."

"Nor do I. It must be difficult indeed to accommodate one with such capricious whims and a general dislike of people."

The earl nodded, but his expression remained guarded. "You have known Miss Longstreet most of your life, I daresay, though scarcely very well. A visit every year or so to Longstreet Manor perhaps?"

"Exactly. And not at all for some years, as she seems to have taken me in aversion as well," Hugh added ruefully.

Lord Westwick's brows rose in surprise. "Has she? But it was not in evidence last evening."

"No, since she's come to Bath, she has accorded me a modicum of cordiality—alongside her standard aspersions on everything and anything I try to do for her."

The older man looked grave. "I don't believe she's ever been to Bath before. I was astonished to learn from your sister that she was here."

"I find it odd myself."

"Well, at least it will give Margaret's daughter a chance to see a little more of the world. Poor thing, stuck up there in Westmorland with few prospects of meeting eligible gentlemen, and none of decent entertainment, given her situation with Rosemarie Longstreet. In the old days, Rosemarie was not so sharp-tongued and displeased with everything."

Lord Westwick fell into a musing state for a moment before shaking his head and saying in a brisker tone, "I had been meaning to consult you about one of my wishes for the horse farm, Sir Hugh. That black of yours—have you ever considered putting him to stud?"

They moved easily into a discussion of horses and said no more on the subject of Miss Longstreet. Before taking his leave, Hugh's glance strayed once again to the crystal display.

Westwick smiled. "You're fascinated by all the sun catchers, eh? They were my wife's idea. A pretty notion, what?"

"It's a charming room. She must have been a very clever woman."

The earl nodded. His eyes focused on one of the crystals, but his thoughts seemed elsewhere. "She was amazing. Whimsical, funny, overflowing with enthusiasm. I had thought to marry a solid country miss, someone of good family, sensible, correct. And then I met Sophie. She changed my life," he said simply.

"You were a lucky man."

"I only wish my luck had held out and that she'd outlived me." Lord Westwick made a dismissive gesture with one hand. "Never mind me. I get a bit maudlin when I'm talking about Sophie. Can't seem to get over her death the way people expect me to."

"Why should you? Pay no attention to the busybodies," Hugh urged, but he was feeling a little out of his depth.

"The minute you put off your black bands, they think you're ready to rejoin society with a vengeance, as though nothing has happened," Lord Westwick said. "In fact, there were those who urged me to parties even before the year was out, saying I would miss a good time all on account of such strict observance. Bah! What do they know?"

When Hugh was once again outside on the pavement, he shook his head ruefully. He had learned nothing about why the earl might be a target for Miss Longstreet's mischief, and he certainly hadn't been able to warn the older man of any danger from that quarter. Hugh would have felt a fool offering such advice to a man who had known his godmother when she was a young woman. It all seemed so unlikely when you stood in that rainbow-filled room, chatting comfortably with an elegant peer of the realm.

Had Miss Armstrong got it all wrong?

Chapter Eight

Nell attempted to forestall a visit from Mr. Bentley by visiting the circulating library on Milsom Street. She carried with her the books that Aunt Longstreet had refused ("a lot of senseless drivel") or completed ("Now, there's a fellow who knows how to describe an historic event"). She herself had read the novel the librarian had recommended, and though she would dearly have loved to discuss it, Emily had yet to return to collect it from her.

It had not occurred to her to suggest that Aunt Longstreet read it. Her aunt had no interest in fiction ("It's all lies, isn't it?"), and in fact had taunted Nell when she sat engrossed in *Mansfield Park*. Nell had little difficulty ignoring her aunt's barbed comments, but when Aunt Longstreet asked what the novel was about, Nell had been a little reluctant to describe the situation. When she had finished the book and closed the last volume with a sigh, her aunt had looked up sharply and said, "I hope that book hasn't given you any romantical notions, Helen."

Nell climbed the stairs to the circulating library with her usual purposeful step, tucking the basket in close to her body so it wouldn't scrape against the walls. She had taken to studying the women she encountered around town, noting their manner of dress and the way in which they wore their hair. It was her intention, on this occasion, to also glance through some of the periodicals about fashion, which the library was certain to carry. Nell had come to believe that she must either look hopelessly provincial, or uncommonly dowdy, to those more versed in the current styles.

The moment she stepped into the large, bright room, Mr. Bentley looked up from his work, as though he sensed her presence. His welcoming smile sat a little uncomfortably on his serious face, but there was no doubt that he was pleased to see her. Nell walked directly to the desk, where she returned his greeting with a cautious one of her own. There were half a dozen patrons in the room, none of whom had paid the least attention to her arrival. Mr. Bentley quizzed her on each book as she lifted it from her basket.

"You haven't brought back the novel?" he asked, surprised.

"No. I finished it two days ago, and loved every word, but I promised Mrs. Holmsly that I would lend it to her. You don't mind, do you?"

"Not at all. She is welcome to it. I'll just make a notation . . ." He pulled a piece of paper over and jotted down a few words. "Can I help you find something today, Miss Armstrong? Perhaps other novels by the same lady?"

"Oh, do you have one? How wonderful. And, Mr. Bentley, I would like to look at some magazines of fashions for ladies, if you would be so good as to point me to them."

"Fashion?" His tone of voice suggested that he could not quite approve of such a choice, but he nonetheless indicated two wooden racks on the north side of the room. "You'll find *La Belle Assemblée* and *Le Beau Monde* over there. The current issues may be with one of the patrons, but they don't circulate, so the older issues will certainly be there."

"Thank you." Nell smiled briefly and crossed to the area he'd indicated. She was quite delighted to find a whole stack of journals. Flipping through the first one to come to hand, she almost gasped at the elegance of the gowns and the modishness of the toilettes of the women. The descriptions of the

fabrics, too, intrigued her, for she found that they were almost entirely light materials, like muslins and satins.

Nell's own gowns were made of heavier, sturdier materials, but she had been aware, from the first moment of arriving in Bath, that she was certainly not in the majority. Even
before the warmer weather of summer came, all the women
about her seemed to be dressed in fabrics that might better
have graced the hottest day of July! Nell had thought it very
strange of them, and had wondered if perhaps Bath had been
enjoying an especially warm spell just prior to her arrival.
But no, these light, gauzy fabrics were what ladies wore
throughout the year, apparently. How very odd of them.

Nell determined on the spot to have one made for herself.

Perusing the most recent issues, she chose exactly what
she wanted, a high-waisted, full-sleeved sprigged muslin
with a mint-green trim at the wrists and neck. How very
charming, she thought. I shall feel like the goddess of
spring!

Knowing that any modiste worth her salt would be able to
duplicate the gown, Nell made a note of the issue and de-
scription as reference. It did occur to her that the modistes in
a town like Bath might be very dear, but she was determined
to have the dress. With no effort at all, she could picture herself walking down a country lane wearing the sprigged
muslin, flowering plums in bloom on either side of her,
wearing slippers of green to match the gown. Oh, there
would be birdsong, and sunshine, and the smell of newly
turned earth.

And perhaps there would be a young man with her.
Someone dressed in the first stare of fashion, very much in
accord with her own appearance. (Mr. Bentley dressed re-
spectably, but certainly not at all fashionably.) Her escort
(who once again looked suspiciously like Sir Hugh) would
pick a newly unfurled blossom for her as they paused by a

stile. (Nell was particularly fond of picturing stiles, as one was often handed over them by one's companion.)

Staring out the window, lost in her daydream, Nell did not notice that Mr. Bentley had approached her. When he cleared his throat, she was abruptly returned to the present. "Ah, Mr. Bentley. You have brought me another book by the author of *Mansfield Park*?"

"Indeed I have. This one is a parody of the more lurid tales of Mrs. Radcliffe and others."

Nell frowned. "A parody? But I had rather have another such as I read before."

"None of her other books are in at the moment, but I will endeavor to hold on to them for you when they are returned."

"Thank you." Nell accepted the volumes he offered her, feeling slightly disappointed.

But time had slipped past, and she had other errands to accomplish. She rose with a shake of her skirts to rid herself of the lingering daydream and her annoyance that Mr. Bentley had interrupted it. She followed the librarian across to his desk to sign for the volumes, and then she proceeded on her way.

Nell's basket was almost full by the time she stopped at a discreet shop on a side street where a modiste's sign— Madame de Vigne—hung beside the door. In the bow window was a gown of superior workmanship and style. Nell stood for a lengthy time contemplating it, and then with determination she pushed open the door. A little bell tinkled to announce her arrival, and it wasn't long before a woman appeared in the archway of the simply furnished room.

"Mademoiselle," the woman said in a heavily accented voice. "How may I be of service to you?"

"I am interested in having a gown made, but there is a certain amount of hurry. I would like it to be ready for Friday evening."

"That would not be impossible," Madame de Vigne admitted, her gaze traveling down the length of Nell's long frame. "What had you in mind?"

"I saw a gown in *La Belle Assemblée* that would be perfect." Nell reached toward the journals she recognized lying on a table, and opened one to the page she had memorized. "This one," she said, tapping the illustration. "I should like it in sprigged muslin, trimmed in a forest green."

The modiste considered the drawing for a while before nodding. "Yes, I could make it, but—forgive me for asking—have you any idea what such a gown would cost?"

Nell felt the color rise to her cheeks. No shopkeeper had ever asked her such a question before. The woman's eyes, she thought now, were critical. Perhaps she regarded Nell's height with disfavor, or she scorned the fact that Nell carried a basket like a country girl, or she found Nell's gown too old-fashioned. "I have no idea what such a gown would cost in Bath," she admitted. "In the country I might have it—material and labor—for under a guinea. I'm sure it must cost more here."

"Indeed it does, mademoiselle. If you provided me with the material early tomorrow morning, I would be able to present you with a finished gown on Friday afternoon for two guineas."

"Two guineas! Goodness." Nell's quarterly allowance from Aunt Longstreet was no more than five pounds. Two guineas seemed an exorbitant amount of money to spend on one dress. And yet . . . Nell really wanted to have a fashionable new gown, just this once. And she would need slippers to go with it. Nell bit her lip, frowning down at the dress design in the journal. "How much is the material likely to cost me?"

Madame de Vigne offered a Gallic shrug. "That would depend upon where you purchased it. You are tall, mademoiselle, so you would need to purchase three yards of the fabric. At Frasiers you might have it for ten shillings, perhaps."

"I see." Nell sadly shook her head. "Thank you, madame, but I believe I won't be able to make such a purchase."

As she turned to leave, Madame de Vigne put a staying hand on her arm. "I have a bolt of cloth, not a sprigged muslin, but it would suit you very well. Wait here."

She disappeared through the archway, and Nell seriously debated whether she shouldn't just leave before the woman returned. But she stood her ground, staring at the long cheval glass across the room, which mirrored her perfectly. Her walking dress did indeed appear dingy in the late afternoon sunlight.

After several minutes, during which Nell scrutinized her reflection more closely than was her wont, the Frenchwoman returned with an emerald-green fabric in her arms. "This," she said, stroking it almost reverently, "is a remnant from a gown I made some months ago. It is too strong a color for most ladies to wear, but I believe you could display it to advantage. But the gown would have to be more . . ."

She waved her expressive hands in the air, shaping and smoothing the outline of a woman's figure. "How would you say it? More simple, less ornate and frilled than the gown you are considering. Let us be honest. You are not in the first blush of youth, mam'selle. The dress you have chosen, it is well enough, I suppose, for the young girl making her come-out. But you, you have a few years of maturity. And your height! *Mon dieu!* You must convince the gentlemen that they admire such stature."

"But I don't imagine they do, madame," Nell suggested.

"Bah! What do they know? Not one gentleman in five understands the first thing about fashion. So, you have only to convince them that only one with your magnificent height could show to advantage such an elegant gown, and voilá! They believe your height is to be admired."

Nell's lips twisted ruefully. "Would that it were so simple, madame. But no matter. The question here is whether I could afford such a gown as you describe, and I very much fear that I could not."

"But that is precisely what you can, and must, do, mam'selle. You cannot go about Bath in such undistinguished garments. No gentleman will take a second look at you."

Nell laughed. "But, madame, I am not interested in having gentlemen take a second look at me."

"Bah!" Madame de Vigne exclaimed again. "Every young woman not yet married is interested in having young gentlemen notice her."

"Then, let us suppose that such is my aim," Nell offered. "That does not change the fact that I am unable to afford a new wardrobe, much less the elegant gown you suggest."

Madame's eyes narrowed, considering her. "But you thought that you could afford one such item for two guineas."

"Well, I was debating the possibility until I realized that I must purchase the fabric, and find myself a pair of matching evening slippers. Much as I should enjoy such a gown, I fear my allowance does not run to so great an expense."

"Then, your allowance is inadequate."

"Quite likely." Nell sighed and stroked the fine emerald satin cloth before regretfully dropping her hand

Madame gave a little puff of disgust. "Then, you must ask for more."

"Madame would not say so if she knew the source of my income." Nell shook her head. "I'm sorry to have taken up so much of your time. "

"Two pounds five shillings, the material included."

"Show me what you have in mind."

Madame searched among the fashion journals and extracted one from the stack. Moistening her index finger, she paged rapidly through until she reached the illustration she sought. "This," she said, tapping it with her finger. "This, in the emerald satin, but without all the ornamentation. A tight corsage, short sleeves slashed in the Spanish style, the robe draped to the side. You would make a very fine figure in it, mam'selle."

Nell told herself it was rash to spend so much of her allowance on one fashionable gown. She reminded herself that she would likely have nowhere to wear the gown once she and Aunt Longstreet returned to Westmorland. She cautioned herself that she would not look so charming in the dress as the model in the illustration did. And she said, "Thank you, madame. I shall have it if you can make it up by Friday."

Friday arrived with a change in the weather. Instead of the sparkling sunlight that had graced the golden stone of Bath for a week, there was a drizzling rain that made everything look sadly bedraggled. Nell had waited as long as she dared before hurrying to Madame de Vigne's, but she had been forced to bring the gown home in a drenching rain.

She hovered as her aunt's dresser, an ancient and stiff-lipped woman, checked the gown for water damage, and sighed when informed that there was none. The dresser, however, regarded Nell with astonishment as she held the gown up for inspection. "And what would you be needing something so fine for, Miss Armstrong?" she asked.

"My aunt and I are going to a concert this evening. She must have mentioned it to you."

"Indeed, but she made no mention of new gowns. I believe she is to wear her half-mourning from after her papa died."

Nell had refused to allow the woman's disapproval to lower her spirits. Tonight, for perhaps the first time in her life, she intended to indulge in a real fantasy—to attend a social function dressed as a proper member of society and escorted by a gentleman of the first stare. That would be a memory to carry back to Westmorland with her, one she could weave daydreams around for years to come, if she chose.

Naturally, Aunt Longstreet had been informed by her dresser of Nell's new gown. When she joined her niece in the parlor, she regarded this confection with a critical eye. "Must have cost you a pretty penny. Don't expect me to be paying for it."

"I won't, Aunt Longstreet."

"Much too dark a color for a girl your age, and plain as a sack. Couldn't afford a few roses or a pearl trim, eh? Better if you hadn't bothered."

"I quite like it, myself," Nell admitted, giving the décolletage a slight tug upward. She was not accustomed to wearing so revealing a gown, though Madame de Vigne had laughed at her concern and said, *"Mon dieu, yours will be the most modest gown there!"*

Any further comment Rosemarie might have made was interrupted by Sir Hugh's arrival. The baronet was impeccably turned out, as always, with shirt points just high enough to give Aunt Longstreet a target for her derogatory remarks. He merely grinned at her and turned toward Nell, where his eyes arrested. It was obvious that he had expected to find her once again sporting her aunt's old-fashioned raiment and that the sight of her in a fashionable gown left him at a loss for words.

At length he bowed and said, "Miss Armstrong. What a charming gown."

"Thank you, Sir Hugh. It's in honor of your arranging our musical evening. It would be a pity to be in Bath and not attend such an event."

"A lot of caterwauling and discordant racket," Rosemarie interposed. "The only decent music ever composed is that to which one can dance."

"An interesting theory," Sir Hugh said. "I'm fond of waltzes myself."

"Waltzes? Nonsense! A flagrant attempt to display the human form in public," Nell's aunt declared. "It's that hussy's German influence."

Nell, not wishing to get into a discussion of the Prince Regent's wife, decided to turn the topic to one of more immediate concern. "Is it still raining, Sir Hugh?"

"Scarcely at all, and my carriage is right outside your door. If you are ready, ladies . . ."

Nell allowed him to drape her ancient pelisse around her shoulders, but she refused to close it tightly, unwilling to crumple her new gown. She wore her only decent jewelry, her grandmother's pearls, and white kid gloves. Madame de Vigne had suggested how to dress her hair: the front in ringlets and the back in plaits fastened with tiny bows of the emerald satin. Mrs. Hodges had helped Nell dye an old pair of white kid shoes a color of green which did not perfectly match the gown, but which seemed perfectly adequate to Nell. Who, after all, was going to pay attention to her shoes?

From the moment they arrived at the concert, Aunt Longstreet appeared to be searching the company for someone. Sir Hugh asked if he might help her to locate anyone in particular, and she snapped that there was not a soul on earth she was interested in seeing. Nell exchanged a sympathetic look with Sir Hugh and took her seat on Sir Hugh's right, as her aunt was on his left. She was keen to hear what he had to say of Mrs. Dorsey but dared not inquire with her aunt so close by.

Nell had never been to so elaborate a concert before. She and her aunt had been invited to small gatherings in their neighborhood where musical entertainments were provided, but these had been simple and usually consisted only of local players. Tonight, the program informed her, there would be a world-famous singer, and the best musicians from all across the country. Her excitement gave a rosy glow to her cheeks, and a luster to her eyes, though she was only conscious of a joyous anticipation of the music and a deep satisfaction with her new gown.

"Will your sister be here this evening?" she asked Sir Hugh.

"No, Emily had other plans. And I am afraid she is not such a lover of music as you are yourself."

"First sensible thing I've heard about her," Rosemarie muttered, but her attention was quickly drawn away by the arrival of a grand dame with three ostrich plumes of such height as to bring down her immediate scorn. "Will you look at that, Helen? Those feathers are taller than the ones your mother and I wore to be presented at court! Pity the poor fellow who sits behind her this evening."

Nell was vastly relieved to see that the woman did not sit down in front of them, but some distance away to their right. Although Aunt Longstreet's voice had not been loud enough for more than their immediate neighbors to hear, Nell was well aware that her aunt would have had no compunction in voicing her displeasure if her view had been blocked— never mind that she might not care to see the singers and the musicians.

Whoever Aunt Longstreet was looking for apparently did not come, as she gave a sniff of annoyance and finally settled back in her chair just as the first musical number was announced. Nell was immediately caught up in the singing. She leaned slightly forward in her seat, intent on the whole experience—the man and woman who sang, the musicians with their sonorous instruments, the glory of the piece itself. When the first selection came to a conclusion, she felt almost stunned with the wonder of all those elements coming together to offer her a far richer musical experience than she had ever had before.

"Tell me," she said, turning to Sir Hugh. "Are all the performances in Bath so fine?"

"Many of them," he admitted, sounding a little bemused. "I am not, I fear, an expert on such matters. At the intermission you will no doubt hear as many unfavorable comments as complimentary ones. It is the nature of Bath society to be critical."

"Well, I shall listen to no one who does not find them quite remarkably good," Nell informed him stoutly. "I may not be an expert, either, but I have never heard anything so beautiful."

Rosemarie had fallen asleep, but as she was not snoring, Nell paid her no heed. In fact, when she had ascertained that her aunt still slept after the second number, which was just as exciting to her as the first, Nell took the opportunity to ask Sir Hugh, in a cautious whisper, if he had learned anything about Mrs. Dorsey.

"I have," he said, after a quick, skeptical glance at his godmother. "Are you quite sure she's asleep?"

"Oh, yes. Music is an unfailing soporific for her."

"Then, I wonder she was willing to come to a concert!"

"She wasn't paying for it," Nell explained, quite seriously.

Sir Hugh shook his head with amusement, but managed to say, "I have actually spoken with Mrs. Dorsey. She is indeed the mother of the fellow I knew some years ago," before their attention was recalled to the musicians once again.

As interested as Nell was in this news, she had no difficulty in concentrating on the concert. It was as easy for her to lose herself in music as in a fantasy. Both served the admirable purpose of transporting her from her rather drab life to an enchanted place where something wonderful could, and often did, happen at any moment. That night, witnessing professional performances beyond her experience, Nell found herself so engrossed that on two occasions tears came to her eyes, which she surreptitiously wiped away with her embroidered handkerchief.

Such sorrows and joys as music spoke of, she thought, resonated with one's own life. The deep wail of the horn reminded her of the despair she had felt after her parents died. The sprightly notes of the flute recalled the delight of winging butterflies and dancing buttercups. Even the anxious whine of the violins felt familiar; she had her own moments of worry about what would become of her. Nell was finding the whole evening an intensely rewarding experience.

Rosemarie roused herself at the intermission to comment, "Thank heaven that's over."

"Not over," Nell informed her. "We are just at the break. Perhaps you would care to stretch your legs."

Her aunt looked disgustedly down at where her legs resided under the half-mourning gown and muttered, "If I am going to move, missy, it will be right out the door."

"Then, by all means retain your seat," Nell said. "I'm thoroughly enjoying the concert, Aunt, and would be very disappointed to leave before it's over."

Aunt Longstreet gave a snort and glared at her, but did no more than wave her away. Sir Hugh, his lips twisted wryly, offered his arm to lead Nell out into the foyer. Amid all the delightful gowns, Nell did not suppose that hers stood out, but she could this once feel a part of the elegant crowd. And if a few gentlemen appeared to notice her, she assured herself that it was only because of her unusual height, or perhaps that she was in company with Sir Hugh.

They stopped not far from the concert room so that Nell could keep her eye on her aunt, who alone remained rigidly seated, her cane gripped in one hand, staring straight ahead. Two older women who were the last to come out of the room appeared to be discussing her.

"I tell you I knew her—years ago. She's John Longstreet's daughter. Inherited every penny from him, too. The other daughter was in disgrace, or maybe dead by then, and no son in the family. This one is godmother to Sir Hugh Nowlin."

Nell was hoping rather desperately that the two women would notice that she and her escort were just within hearing range of their gossip, but the other woman, unaware, had her eyes on her companion. She nodded vigorously, and said, "I hear he has grand expectations there. And they can't come too soon, I imagine. His father all but ruined Fallings."

Chapter Nine

Nell's hand had unconsciously tightened on Sir Hugh's arm. Color rose to her cheeks, and she was unable to meet his eyes. In one skillful movement he turned her so they were facing in a different direction, away from the two ladies and their distressing revelations. He said nothing but with narrowed eyes studied the crowd before them. Eventually his face relaxed into a smile, and he said, "Let me introduce you to Mrs. Billings. She's Holmsly's sister, and therefore Emily's sister-in-law. No two women could be more different, but they are the best of friends."

With that he moved them carefully through the throng until they reached a diminutive redheaded woman who greeted Nell's escort with affection.

"Sir Hugh! It is almost as rare to find you here as it would be your sister," she teased.

"We Nowlins don't do well at sitting still for so long," he admitted. "Mrs. Billings, I don't believe you've met Miss Armstrong. She's my godmother's niece. They've come to Bath for a few weeks so that Miss Longstreet may take the waters."

"How delightful! Emily has mentioned you," Mrs. Billings said, with a warm smile. "Are you enjoying the concert, Miss Armstrong?"

"Very much. Everything about it seems wonderful. But

Sir Hugh tells me that the concertgoers will find fault with it, so no doubt I am hopelessly provincial."

"Or our concertgoers are hopelessly jaded," suggested Mrs. Billings. Her brow creased slightly. "Or perhaps it is that we have come to expect such a high level of performance that anything less than perfection is something to be noted. In either case, Miss Armstrong, I trust such comments, should you chance to hear them, will not detract from your enjoyment."

Nell's enjoyment had been dampened by her chance overhearing of something else entirely, but she declared stoutly that they would not. To change the direction of this conversation, she asked, "Perhaps you could direct me to where in town I might find the music for that third piece, Mrs. Billings."

Though Nell had looked forward to speaking alone with Sir Hugh during the intermission, she found herself clinging to Mrs. Billings so that she would not have to either pretend she had not heard those two dreadful women, or discuss the meaning of their comments with the baronet. The comments had shaken her, and she did not want to let on that she had been discomposed. Aunt Longstreet had frequently put her to the blush, heaven knew. But there was something quite different about tonight's revelation.

It was with relief that Nell seated herself for the second half of the concert. She was unable to pay full attention to the music, as distracting thoughts wandered through her mind. Foremost among these was the understanding that Sir Hugh might not have been the best person to confide in about her worries.

Rosemarie was drowsy but awake on the carriage drive back to Queen Square, so there was no chance for any private discourse. In the entry hall that irascible woman commented, "All that screeching has given me the headache. I'm ready for my bed." And she shuffled across the entry hall and began to climb the stairs without a backward glance.

Nell turned to the butler, who had just relieved her of her pelisse, and said, "That will be all, thank you, Woodbridge. I'll see Sir Hugh out."

"Very good, miss."

The moment Woodbridge had disappeared down the hall, Sir Hugh turned to Nell and said, "I'm sorry you were forced to hear those two women tonight, Miss Armstrong, but you should know that what they said was largely the truth."

"I see."

He gave a tsk of frustration. "It's all such an awkward business, and one which is indelicate in the extreme to discuss. My godmother has every right to dispose of her property in any manner of her choosing. That goes without saying. But what must be recognized is that an expectation of my inheriting her estate has grown up over the years."

Nell raised a hand to stay his confession. "Sir Hugh, my grandfather intended the property should go to you after Aunt Longstreet. He did not wish me to have it, as he believed me to be illegitimate." She turned toward the door, hoping that he would follow.

But the baronet stood rooted to the spot. "Nonsense," he said flatly.

"My parents," she said, a catch in her voice, "were both brilliantly irresponsible and careless. They were also delightful, loving people. Really, you must be leaving now, Sir Hugh. Else Woodbridge will be concerned."

Sir Hugh shook his head in frustration. "But, Miss Armstrong, you were still his granddaughter. He should have made provision for you."

"He took me in. Longstreet Manor has been my home for many years."

"Does your aunt believe in your legitimacy?"

Nell tilted her chin up. "She has never said, one way or the other. But my aunt is fond of me."

"Then, she should be willing to provide for you."

"My grandfather did not wish me to inherit any part of his estate, and I'm sure my aunt will carry out his wishes."

"That is a terrible hold she has over you."

"You are mistaken."

"Then, why do you stay with her?"

"Where else could I go? Besides, I promised my grandfather on his deathbed that I would always stay with Aunt Longstreet, and I shall."

"He cannot have expected you to give up your life to serve your aunt."

"Oh, but he did." Nell had no difficulty in picturing that scene, when her grandfather lay in his four-poster bed, weakened by days of bloodletting and no appetite for food. His hands had become shrunken, but he had held onto her with an unexpected strength. "Promise me," he had demanded. "Promise me you won't ever leave your aunt."

And Nell had promised. What choice had she had, after all? He had given her a home when she had nowhere to go, had fed and clothed her. And all in spite of the fact that he had cast off her mother and did not accept the legitimacy of his granddaughter. Yes, he had known what he was asking of her.

To forestall any more questions from the baronet, she turned to the door and opened it. "Really, it's late, Sir Hugh."

"Of course." He grasped and pressed her hand briefly before stepping out onto the stoop. "Oh, I almost forgot. Mrs. Dorsey lives in Corn Street, and she is indeed the mother of the young man I knew some years ago. Good night, Miss Armstrong."

"Good night, Sir Hugh."

Though she shut the door immediately, Nell remained

standing in the entry hall for some time. She could almost feel the pressure of his fingers on her hand, and see the intensity of his blue eyes on her face. You will not develop a *tendre* for him, she warned herself. That would be foolish beyond permission.

Not only did her own situation preclude anything developing between the two of them, but his motives for paying the slightest attention to her were surely suspect. Sir Hugh wanted—nay, needed—to know where he stood with regard to inheriting Longstreet Manor from his godmother, because he was in need of that inheritance.

With a ragged sigh, Nell moved toward the stairs, remembering as her emerald gown swayed with her how regal she had felt earlier in the evening. Well, the gown at least she would always have—even if she had nowhere to wear it once they returned to Longstreet Manor.

Chapter Ten

Sir Hugh irritably tapped his curly beaver hat down over his forehead, dismissed his carriage, and strode off along Queen Square. Hell of a sensitive subject for the two of them to be discussing, but what choice had he had? He could scarcely have avoided it after they'd overheard the two women gossiping about his inheritance at the concert.

Hugh had tried to be honest with Miss Armstrong about his situation, and she had, he believed, responded with just as much frankness. She apparently found it perfectly reasonable that his godmother would leave the entire estate to Sir Hugh. Yet he now found that position incomprehensible, given that Miss Armstrong had served as companion to her aunt for ten long years.

Understanding the workings of a mind such as Rosemarie Longstreet's was well beyond Sir Hugh's powers. He was himself a straightforward man, and a good-natured one. He could not easily decipher the contradictory directions of a perverse mind such as Miss Longstreet's. And though she had lived with her for so long, Miss Armstrong might not be correct about his godmother's intentions and expectations, either.

And damned if he knew how he felt about Miss Armstrong's—Nell's—own revelations. Never leave her aunt? Impossible. Nell had looked so striking in the fashionable emerald gown, so regal and captivating, that Hugh could no longer envision her banished to the wilds of Westmorland with his difficult godmother. Nell deserved the opportunity to make a life for herself, to enjoy the society and culture of Bath and London, to surround herself with people who could offer her pleasurable outings and sensible conversation.

But Hugh found himself in an impossible position with regard to Nell. He was intrigued by her, attracted to her, and wary of her. He felt a considerable urge to unlock for her all the pleasures of Bath and its surrounds. Yet he feared that he would be perceived—by the woman herself, as well as her aunt and every other member of Bath society—as merely self-serving.

And how serious was she about this promise to her grandfather? Surely a woman of sense would not hold herself bound forever to a crotchety aunt merely because her grandfather had extracted such a promise. Sir Hugh could only wonder whether Miss Longstreet even knew of the constraint.

There were other questions in his mind as well. Why hadn't his godmother gotten in touch with Mrs. Dorsey? For that matter, why did she hate Lord Westwick? There was even the question of whether the estimable Mr. Bentley was pursuing Nell for love or money. Or was that pursuit merely a figment of his sister Emily's imagination?

Sir Hugh's head had begun to spin with the plethora of unanswered questions. The only thing he knew for certain was that he planned to escort the Queen Square ladies to another assembly, because he had every intention of standing up with Nell in that fetching emerald gown.

For the time being he refused to consider how she was going to learn to dance.

"You look a little peaked this morning," Rosemarie remarked at breakfast.

"Do I?" Nell glanced in the mirror across the table from

where she sat, but she saw nothing different about her face. "I so enjoyed the concert last night."

Her aunt gave a snort but said, "Well, I'm glad you did. A lot of caterwauling, to my mind. And I can't think half the people were there for anything more than to see and be seen."

"Perhaps," Nell agreed diplomatically.

"You won't find much use for that new gown."

"Perhaps not."

"Must have spent a fortune on it."

"Mmmm." Nell sipped her tea, then spread butter on her toast.

"I want you to take a note 'round to Mrs. Dorsey this morning."

Nell almost dropped the piece of toast. "Mrs. Dorsey? Why, of course, Aunt. Does she live close by?"

"Corn Street. Doesn't sound a very promising direction, but according to the map it's not far." Rosemarie dug in her pocket and came up with a sealed missive. "Right after breakfast, mind."

"Certainly. And shall we expect her for tea later?"

Her aunt gave an irritable shrug. "Depends on whether she's available, does it not? Wait for her answer. And, Helen, there's no need to tell her how long we've been in town. I just mentioned that we'd needed a few days to settle in."

"I see." Nell slipped the note into her own pocket. If it had not been sealed, she would have been sore tempted to read it, except that she doubted her aunt had revealed anything of significance. "Have you any other errands for me to run this morning, Aunt?"

Her aunt regarded her suspiciously. "Why? Planning to gad about town are you?"

Nell shook her head with amusement. "As usual, Aunt Longstreet."

"None of your lip, Helen. And another thing. I will want

to be private with Gertrude. I'll thank you to excuse yourself from tea."

"As you wish, Aunt."

Now that, Nell decided, could only mean trouble. Definitely Aunt Longstreet was up to mischief. There was no other reason for her to exclude Nell from tea with her old friend. It behooved Nell to find out as much as she could before that tea even occurred.

So as soon as breakfast was finished, she put on her bonnet and pelisse and sallied forth. The weather had cleared somewhat, but remained overcast, the skies leaden and the air on the chill side. Nell walked past the Westgate Buildings and saw the Hetling pump, but instead of heading toward the abbey, she turned toward the quay. The near end of Corn Street was reached by Peter Street, and she walked at only a moderate pace, as she did not wish to arrive at an unreasonably early hour.

The house whose number she sought was modest but pleasant, built of the city's usual golden stone and well maintained. There was a brass knocker on the door, which Nell plied with more assurance than she felt. When a maid answered the door, Nell explained her errand was to deliver the message from Rosemarie Longstreet, and to await an answer, if that was possible.

"Oh, yes, miss," the girl said, dropping a little curtsy. "Mistress is just in the morning room with her correspondence. I'll show you in."

Nell followed her down a narrow hallway to a room at the back which was filled with so many plants that it looked more like a conservatory than a sitting room. At a desk near the multipaned windows sat an elderly woman in a white cap. Mrs. Dorsey looked so much older than Aunt Longstreet that Nell was startled for a moment, knowing that the two women were essentially the same age.

Not that Mrs. Dorsey looked ill, but there was an air of

fragility to her quite unlike Aunt Longstreet's peppery vigor. The maid announced her as "Miss Armstrong, niece to Miss Longstreet," and the little woman perked up instantly.

"Oh, then she's come!" She rose to her feet with some difficulty, but walked steadily across the room toward Nell. "And you are the niece of whom she's written so often. How pleased I am to meet you at last."

"As I am to meet you," Nell assured her. She handed Mrs. Dorsey the note, saying, "Aunt Longstreet asked that I await a reply, if possible. I believe she's hoping you will come to visit us in Queen Square."

"Please, sit down. Lucy will bring us a cup of tea."

Ordinarily Nell would have refused such an offer so shortly after her meal, but she had every intention of learning what she could from Mrs. Dorsey, and that would require spending time with her. She accepted the seat her hostess suggested, a chair tucked closely beside a broadleafed plant whose name Nell requested.

"Why, that's an aspidistra," Mrs. Dorsey explained. "My son has taken to bringing me a different plant each time he visits, and I've become that fond of them. Now they're something of a pastime of mine. I learn about their care from an old gardener friend down the block."

"They're lovely," Nell said, meaning it. "They make the room feel almost like an outdoor park."

Mrs. Dorsey nodded enthusiastically. "Have a look about you while I read your aunt's note," she suggested.

But Nell scarcely had time to turn around before Mrs. Dorsey was exclaiming, "Oh, I should love to come for tea this afternoon! I'm delighted Rosemarie is here in Bath. And Queen Square is such a lovely spot. Fancy her not letting me know when she was to arrive!"

"I'm sure she didn't want you to feel any obligation to see us settled in," Nell offered. "My aunt is a very independent woman."

"Ah, yes, I remember that." Mrs. Dorsey nodded reminiscently. "There were those who were surprised at her engagement, you know, as they believed Rosemarie was unlikely to welcome any man ruling over her."

Her engagement? Nell felt a prickle of excitement, but forced herself to appear calm. "But you weren't surprised, yourself?"

"No, no. I always suspected she had a *tendre* for Westwick. Oh, he was a striking-looking man in those days. Came from her neighborhood, too. Seemed an entirely appropriate match."

Lord Westwick had been engaged to Rosemarie Longstreet? Nell had to bite her lip to keep from exclaiming aloud: What happened? Instead she nodded knowledgeably and fingered the leaf that was curling near her head, hoping Mrs. Dorsey would continue in this vein. But the older woman just sighed and said, "Ah, well," before perking up and adding, "Please tell your aunt that I shall be delighted to come this afternoon. I hope I'll see you there, Miss Armstrong."

Nell rose, saying, "Yes, indeed. Aunt Longstreet will be so pleased that you can make it."

Out on the street she stood in stunned, oblivious dismay as a dray passed alarmingly close by. Aunt Longstreet had been engaged to Lord Westwick. Impossible. Or so one would have supposed. What could have happened? Since a gentleman could not cry off, it must have been Aunt Longstreet who did so. But why? Nell could hardly imagine a more desirable husband than Lord Westwick would have been as a young man.

Could Mrs. Dorsey be mistaken? The elderly woman had shown no sign of being less than mentally capable, but older people sometimes had odd skips in their memories, didn't they? Nell considered the few minutes she'd spent with her aunt's old friend and concluded it was highly unlikely that

Mrs. Dorsey could have made up an engagement between Rosemarie Longstreet and the Earl of Westwick out of whole cloth. There was, of course, the possibility that Aunt Longstreet had lied in a letter to her friend about having attached the earl, and then gone on to repudiate her betrothal. That, however, did not sound much like the Aunt Longstreet with whom Nell was familiar.

As she began her walk back to Queen Square, Nell mulled over what she knew of the earl, but it was really very little. Certainly in their perusal of the Peerage, she and her aunt had never read about him, nor had her aunt ever so much as mentioned him before their arrival in Bath. Now Aunt Longstreet was insisting that Nell have nothing to do with him, though she would give no explanation.

When Nell arrived at Queen Square, she discovered Emily Holmsly climbing the stair to their door. The young matron's retinue had not accompanied her on this occasion, and she caught a glimpse of Nell before plying the knocker. "Oh, capital!" she exclaimed. "Just the person I wanted to see. Will you accompany me to the Pump Room, Nell?"

Nell was about to refuse when the possibility of obtaining information from this charming young lady occurred to her. "Yes, if you'll just allow me to give Woodbridge a message."

"But of course."

Emily was adjusting the set of her bonnet when Nell slipped back out of the house after informing the butler that Mrs. Dorsey would be coming for tea. Nell had never seen such a delightful confection as the rose-colored lutestring bonnet, saucily turned up in front, that her visitor wore. She was contemplating how much Madame de Vigne would charge for such an item when Emily linked arms with her and confided, "I detest going into the Pump Room alone, you know. To be sure, before I have taken three steps there are half a dozen acquaintances there to greet me, but walking in the door alone simply unnerves me."

Nell found this hard to believe, given her new friend's sociable nature, but it was certainly an emotion with which she could identify. "My aunt has taken to avoiding the Pump Room, and I cannot say that I am displeased. Not only did we have no acquaintance there, but she was given to finding fault with the arrangements, to say nothing of the taste of the waters."

"Ah, but does she not believe in their curative power?"

"I doubt it, yet she sends Woodbridge to the Hetling pump for a glass now and again. And coincidently, her gout has eased considerably over the past week."

Emily cocked her head mischievously. "There, you see? Cured by the waters."

Nell laughed. "Perhaps. In any case, as she is more comfortable now, her disposition has improved. If I have the Bath waters to thank for that, I can only be grateful."

"Yes, indeed." Emily reached into her reticule and withdrew a tiny green satin bow. "Is this yours? Hugh brought it by first thing. He said it was discovered in his carriage this morning. I know he took you and Miss Longstreet to the concert last night."

Nell accepted the bow with a small stab of disappointment. Sir Hugh could have brought it to her himself, had he chosen to. Instead, he had delegated his sister. "Yes, I wore several in my hair last night. They matched my gown."

Emily's eyes sparkled. "Hugh said it was a spectacular gown. Oh, I wish I could have seen it. Not at all like the gown you wore to the Upper Rooms, apparently."

"No, it was new, made up by a woman here in Bath." Nell thought it unlikely Sir Hugh had called it a "spectacular" gown; that was just Emily's hyperbole. "I shall probably never have another chance to wear it, but I don't regret hav-

ng it made. I felt truly fashionable for the first time in my
life."

"Well, we shall just have to look for other occasions on
which you may sport it," Emily suggested. "A ravishing
gown should not be allowed to molder away in the closet."

Nell merely nodded. She was now familiar with Emily's
penchant for trying to solve any problem that arose in her
vicinity, and she didn't want to give her an excuse for doing
something on Nell's behalf. "You missed a delightful concert last night," she said. "Your brother hinted that you're
not overfond of music."

"Mmm. Not unless it is music to which I can dance,"
Emily agreed, her smile mischievous. "I am hopelessly un-
cultured, you see."

"I never would have suspected," Nell assured her with an
answering grin. "Do you not play the pianoforte and dabble
in watercolors?"

"Well, as to that, I suppose I am moderately accomplished. Because, you see, it is my own performance which
is being put to the test when I am asked to play, or when
someone observes a watercolor of mine. Fortunately, I am
able to play what pieces I please, or draw what object interests me, so it is not at all the same as appreciating the accomplishments of others."

"I see. Do you not enjoy the accomplishments of others?"

Emily cocked her head to one side, considering. "Not in
the way other people do, I fear. I have no discrimination. If
the music is lively, I exult in it. If the painting is cheerful, I
feel a warm glow. On the other hand, if the music is lugubri-
ous, or the painting downright depressing, my spirits are
lowered, and I cannot value those artistic merits which others find so obvious."

Nell stepped over a stone which was blocking their path
while Emily skipped around it. "Well, that doesn't sound
like such an awful thing to me," she admitted.

Emily lifted her dainty shoulders in a shrug. "No, but it means I am denied that uplifting thrill other people feel when they listen to beautifully trained voices or they examine the works of some old master painter. Still," she added happily, "I seem to survive without it. My joys come from simpler pleasures—my baby's smile, the babble of a sunny brook, the feel of the music inside me when I'm dancing. That's enough for me."

"I should think it would be enough for anyone."

"Well, they're not sophisticated pleasures, but I shall just have to do without those. Or perhaps, when I am an old lady, I shall acquire some taste for them, or pretend that I have, so my grandchildren won't be ashamed of me."

Nell shook her head at Emily's nonsense, though she couldn't help but wonder out loud, "Do you suppose those women at the concert last night who could find nothing good to say about the music were only pretending to be knowledgeable? Or were their ears so finely tuned that they could detect the smallest error?"

"I suppose," Emily said with some asperity, "that they were people who are prone to criticize, and have too little refinement to restrain themselves in public."

They had reached the Pump Room, and Emily linked her arm with Nell's as they entered the large room. "Now, you are to stay with me, if you please. I do not wish to have some gentleman thinking he can separate me from my friend for a tête-à-tête in the corner. One or two of these so-called gentlemen would attempt to do just that, if one allowed them to."

"I don't think any gentleman has ever attempted to do such a thing to me," Nell said.

Emily rolled her eyes. "Well, of course not, silly. You are always here with your aunt!"

However, the first gentleman to approach them was Lord Westwick, and Nell felt her face flushing at the memory of what Mrs. Dorsey had told her. The earl appeared not to notice anything unusual as he greeted them with a charming bow. "Ladies, how delightful to find you here, just when I thought I had come too late to encounter any of my acquaintance."

"Too late! Why, it's the earliest I have been here all month," Emily informed him.

"Ah, perhaps that is the problem. I shall have to delay my entrance to a more fashionable hour." He offered each of them an arm, suggesting a walk about the room.

Nell felt slightly nervous with the earl now, but she imagined her discomfort would be attributed to shyness or an unfamiliarity with the social niceties of the Pump Room. Emily had no hesitation in flirting outrageously with their escort, since he was of an age to be her father, if not her grandfather. And Emily's artless chatter would have covered for Nell's own quietness, had not the earl made a point of including her in the conversation.

"Have you formed the habit of coming late to the Pump Room, too, Miss Armstrong?" he asked with teasing interest.

"Why, no, we haven't been coming at all for the last week or so. And when we came, it was much earlier than this."

"Your aunt is an early riser, is she?"

The question seemed somehow embarrassing to Nell. If he had married Rosemarie Longstreet, he would know such things. "Yes, no, well, here in Bath she rises later than at Longstreet Manor. But she has decided against attending the Pump Room."

"Too bad, for I imagine that limits your own ventures here."

"Oh, I don't mind at all. I find the waters peculiarly nasty."

The earl laughed. "You and everyone else. But there are those who swear by them. And it has always been my impression that most people come here for the company, and not the waters."

"Yes, indeed!" Emily agreed. "I doubt if half the people even try them after the first time."

"But your aunt came to Bath for the waters, didn't she?" Lord Westwick asked.

Nell thought he was regarding her rather closely, as if her answer was of some import to him. She tried to reply in a circumspect manner, so as not to lie. "My aunt occasionally suffers from the gout and had heard that the waters were especially good as a cure for her illness."

"Ah, someone recommended them to her," he surmised.

"I believe so," she said carefully.

"Has she been here before?"

"No, she seldom leaves the Manor."

"Mmmm." The earl seemed to consider this for a moment before he asked, "And do you get away from the Manor much, Miss Armstrong?"

"No, never," Nell admitted with a flush.

"Never!" Emily exclaimed. "Oh, you poor dear! Well, we shall have to make a change in that."

Nell shook her head with amused frustration. "Emily, my dear, the Manor is my home. It is not so strange that I don't travel, especially without my aunt. She is in need of my companionship."

"Ha!" Emily gave a spirited toss of her head. "In need of companionship, is she? The woman isn't fit for human society. Do you know, Lord Westwick, that she wasn't at all accommodating to my dear little boy? Why, she practically pushed us out the door!"

Lord Westwick's eyes twinkled. "Did she, my dear? I must admit that she did the same to me."

Emily stared at him, aghast. "Surely not!"

"Indeed. Miss Armstrong was there and can verify that I received a very poor reception."

Nell frowned slightly but nodded. "My aunt takes peculiar aversions from time to time." Carefully, avoiding the earl's gaze, she said, "But it is exceedingly strange to me that she would behave so with a gentleman from our own neighborhood."

"Is it?" he challenged. "Does she not behave in a similar way to your neighbors at home?"

"Well, as to that . . ." Nell's lips twitched. "Most of them, my lord, know better than to come and visit us!"

"My word!" Emily cried. "And now you tell us that not only are you stuck in that godforsaken manor, but that none of your neighbors come to visit. I tell you, Nell, that it is insupportable. Something must be done."

"There is nothing to be done," Nell told her firmly. "I am perfectly content with my situation."

"Perfectly content!" Emily fumed. "My dear, if you are perfectly content, you must be all about in your head. And that, I know you are not!"

Lord Westwick stepped in to distract attention from Nell's situation. "I think, Miss Armstrong, that you have no access to a mount while you are in Bath, and I should be happy to correct that. You may have heard that I have a small horse farm not far from town. Perhaps you could drive there with me this afternoon, and we could choose an appropriate horse for you to ride."

"How . . . how kind of you," Nell said. "That would be most appreciated, Lord Westwick."

When Emily attempted to resurrect her previous indignation, Nell saw Lord Westwick give her a quelling stare, and the young matron fell silent. For this Nell could only be thankful. She did not wish to be viewed as the object of pity by such a dashing young lady—or by anyone, for that matter. She entered enthusiastically into the earl's discussion of the differences in riding occasioned by the disparate terrains of Westmorland and Somerset, and eventually Emily joined in as well. But there was still that martial light in her eyes which alarmed Nell. Mightn't she approach her brother about her discoveries? Nell was horrified by the thought of Sir Hugh's pity.

Lord Westwick arranged to call for Nell in his carriage early in the afternoon. The timing was ideal, as it would provide her with an excuse for not being there when Mrs. Dorsey called. She would not, of course, tell her aunt with whom she was to be. No sense in distressing her unnecessarily. But the opportunity to find out more about the earl intrigued Nell, and the chance to ride gave her a sense of country freedom she had not experienced since their arrival in Bath.

Chapter Eleven

It was not Lord Westwick, however, who called for her. Nell had waited anxiously close to the front door in order to avoid having her aunt catch a glimpse of the earl. When there was a clatter of hooves in the street outside the Queen Square house, Nell hastened to tie the old-fashioned bonnet into place. Her even older riding habit, she had decided, was not really a disgrace, as its lines were classic and it fit her well. As the brass knocker sounded and their butler opened the door, she stepped forward, only to be confronted with Sir Hugh.

"Oh," she said, startled. "I'm sorry, Sir Hugh. I am expecting Lord Westwick to call for me any moment."

"I have convinced him to forego that pleasure," Sir Hugh said, bowing. "I hope you will not mind, Miss Armstrong, but I offered to convey you in my curricle, so that he might go ahead and see that all was in readiness for your visit."

"How kind," she murmured. "A curricle, you say? I've never ridden in a curricle. Shall I be safe?"

Sir Hugh looked rueful. "I cannot speak for any other driver on the road, but I assure you I shall do my utmost to deliver you safe to the farm."

"Of course." Nell preceded him down to where a tiny older man in livery was standing at the horse's head. The little elf pulled his forelock in polite recognition, and Sir Hugh assisted Nell into the sporting vehicle. The baronet then climbed in beside her, picked up the reins, and nodded to the elf, who hastened to the back of the curricle and clambered on just as Sir Hugh gave his horse the order to start. Nell, accustomed to closed carriages and slow starts, gave an involuntary exclamation of surprise and grabbed hold of the seat to keep herself upright.

"I beg your pardon," Sir Hugh apologized, but his attention was mainly on the street before them. There were pedestrians crossing near the square, and a handsome large carriage that took up most of the street. The situation seemed fraught with danger to Nell, but Sir Hugh managed to avoid running down any walker, or grazing the side of the carriage. She let her breath out with a sigh.

He glanced over at her, a grin stretching his generous mouth. "Frightened you, did I? You have my permission to keep your eyes closed until we're in open country if you wish, Miss Armstrong."

"No, no. Then I would miss all the fascinating sites. Look, there's Mr. Bentley on his way to the library. And isn't that Emily Holmsly's sister-in-law?"

For answer, Sir Hugh lifted his hat in salute to the young lady as they drove past, which necessitated his using only one hand on the reins. Nell was tempted to ask him to not do that again, but knew better than to protest. She merely gritted her teeth together for the duration of their wending their way through the crowded streets of Bath, and relaxed only when they at last reached open countryside. Past Southgate Street and across the Old Bridge, they reached Holloway, with its steep ascent up to Beechen Cliff. Sir Hugh guided his curricle onto the winding Prospect Place and brought the vehicle to a gentle halt.

"What do you think of that?" he asked, gesturing to the city of Bath spread out beneath them. Nell could see the Avon winding through town, and the magnificent Abbey towering over the buildings around it. Sir Hugh pointed out the surrounding landmarks—Lansdown Hill, Kelston Round Hill, Englishcombe

Barrow. To Nell it was a glorious sight, and she said as much. Gratified, he smiled warmly on her and remarked, "I have always felt this was one of the most delightful prospects in the area. But we should be on our way. We're headed in the direction of Combe Down, just beyond Glasshouse Farm."

Once the dangerous traffic was behind them, Nell allowed herself to enjoy her excursion with the baronet. They chatted easily about life in the country, about the baronet's horses, about the music they'd heard the previous evening—the usual mix of comfortable conversation that slid from topic to topic when two people had many interests in common. Nell did not bring her aunt's name into the conversation, nor did Sir Hugh mention her.

As they bowled along country lanes, the scenery about them shifted to rolling hills dotted with trees in new leaf. A warm spring breeze carried the rich scent of plowed earth. Nell stole circumspect glances at her companion, admiring the openness of his countenance and the humor in his eyes. Her heart swelled with an unfamiliar emotion that made her want to laugh and cry at the same time. She wanted to rest her head on his broad shoulder, to have his strong arms close around her, to feel the wild touch of his lips on hers.

And not in one of her daydreams.

She wanted this charming, thoughtful man to cherish her, to love her. Nell had never desired that of a man in her life. Scold herself as she might for such folly, she had to acknowledge that she *did* want these things from Sir Hugh. That would be her secret, tucked firmly away in her heart, for her alone to treasure. It didn't matter that there was no possibility of her achieving such a goal. Sitting beside him, talking with him, marveling at the sheer beauty of the day, was enough for her now.

Because she was distracted, she only belatedly noticed the solitary figure on horseback. Even from some distance there was something about the cut of his shoulders and the tilt of his head that gave her the sense that she recognized him.

Sir Hugh had been pointing out the approaching farm and had not as yet appeared to notice the horseman. Just as Nell suddenly exclaimed, "Why, I believe that's Mr. Holmsly!" the rider abruptly wheeled his horse, caused him to leap a shallow ditch, and took off across the field beyond.

Startled, Sir Hugh followed the line of her pointing finger and frowned at the disappearing rider. "John Holmsly? Emily's husband? I can't think why he should be here."

"I can't think why he should take off like that."

"But I fear you must be mistaken, Miss Armstrong. It is my understanding that John is in Bristol at present."

"Perhaps he is on his way back."

"We're quite a distance from the road to Bristol. This lane leads only to Lord Westwick's farm and two other country places. It doesn't even connect with any other road."

"Well, the man looked a great deal like Emily's husband," Nell stubbornly insisted.

"There's more than one handsome devil wandering about the English countryside," he quizzed her. "It was probably a local estate agent come to survey something in the acreage over that hill. There's probably no other access to it than across the fields."

Unconvinced, Nell nevertheless said no more on the subject. Instead she pointed to two fine-looking horses racing along beside the road. "Will these be Lord Westwick's horses?"

"They will. On the knoll there you can just make out the farmhouse behind the trees. It's not a large place, but well-appointed. The earl has spent a great deal of time here since his wife died. I'm sure it's what helped him get through that loss. They were an especially devoted couple."

"Does he breed horses for racing?"

"Mostly, though oddly he seems not much interested in the races themselves. He's particularly talented at choosing which horses are natural runners, and which would be best trained as carriage or riding horses. He has some of the finest hacking horses I've ever ridden."

Sir Hugh guided his horse off the lane and onto the drive up to the farmhouse, which was built of the same warm stone as the buildings in Bath. It was, as Sir Hugh had said, a modest structure, but it was somehow welcoming in a way a more formal dwelling would not have been. Longstreet Manor, for instance, had always seemed stiff and uncompromising to Nell. As one approached it, there were no shrubs or vines to distract from the hard lines, no graceful trees to soften the vertical expanse of stone, no flowers to brighten the grim grayness of the place.

Combe Park was far otherwise. Ancient elms flanked its sides, and there were flower beds in every direction. Though it was still too early for any but the first of the spring flowers to be in blossom, Nell could picture the house at the height of summer. What a glorious vision that would be! As Sir Hugh handed her down from the curricle, Lord Westwick came around the side of the building in his riding clothes.

"Excellent! I knew you'd arrive in good time with Sir Hugh handling the ribbons. Welcome to Combe Park, Miss Armstrong. Will you allow me to show you around?"

Their tour of the house and the barns and outbuildings took over an hour. Nell was delighted with what she saw, and intrigued by the earl's obvious pride and pleasure in the property. And though he referred frequently to having an excellent manager for his horse business, they never met the man, and Nell suspected that Lord Westwick was himself responsible for the thriving nature of his endeavors. She had never seen so many fine animals in one place in her life.

"So, which is it to be?" the earl asked at length. "Miss Ginny is gentle and mild-mannered. Socrates is much more spirited, but would not unseat a lady, no matter what the provocation. Now, Lightning here is fast and unpredictable. I think perhaps Sir Hugh might enjoy that challenge."

As Sir Hugh bowed his head in acknowledgment, Nell walked back to a loose box they had passed a few minutes previously. The horse within thrust her head over the gate and gave Nell a push with her nose. The sign on the loose box designated her as "Rising Star," and she was an unusual shade of gray. Nell rubbed the horse's forehead. "Tell me about her," she suggested.

Lord Westwick gave Nell a sharp look. "We've had a little trouble with her," he admitted. "She's fast, but she doesn't like the stable lads riding her. She doesn't throw them; she just doesn't cooperate."

"Could I ride her?"

The earl looked torn. "If you'll excuse me, I have to admit I have my doubts. I have no idea how well you ride, my dear, and Rising Star is, as I say, a bit troublesome."

"I have been told that I ride as well as my mother did."

The earl's gaze narrowed. "As well as Margaret? Who told you that?"

"Finch. Did you know him?"

"I did, though he had only recently been hired when . . . Well, you may try Rising Star if you wish. Most likely she won't try to throw you."

Sir Hugh had listened to this interchange with apparent interest. For a moment Nell thought that he might object. She met his gaze with a questioning one of her own, and he merely shrugged and said, "Then, we shall both be on challenging horses, Miss Armstrong."

Lord Westwick had three horses saddled as he was joining them on his favorite mount, a bay gelding named Whisper. Rising Star objected to the bridle and she objected to the sidesaddle, but she eventually accepted both. Before allowing the earl to toss her up onto the horse, Nell stood for several minutes stroking and talking to Rising Star, whose ears flicked wildly back and forth. When Nell was eventually seated firmly in the sidesaddle, Rising Star danced sideways for a minute before settling down. Nell found the two gentlemen watching her anxiously.

"Come, she'll do better if we work out her fidgets," Nell informed them serenely. "Surely she would rather have a good run than amble about the paddock."

"Undoubtedly," Lord Westwick agreed. "So, if you are ready . . ."

Because the farm was used for breeding, raising, and training a variety of horses, there were many trails and tracks in the area. Nell was especially enchanted by the one they took, which skirted a lake for half a mile, and then plunged into a wood where the sunlight filtered dazzlingly through the trees. The three galloped along the lake, slowed their horses through the wood, and once again raced across an unplanted field as they circled back toward the stables.

Rising Star was an exhilarating ride. None of the horses at Longstreet Manor had her speed or sheer vitality. Nell could tell her control over the animal was tenuous; there was a streak of wildness in Rising Star. But at each point when she might have broken free, the mare allowed herself to be drawn back by Nell's firm hand on the reins. That, too, was an exciting experience.

When Nell climbed down in the stable yard, she was glowing from her adventure. Lord Westwick, who had assisted her to alight, said, "She's yours."

Nell stared at him. "I . . . I don't understand."

"I'm giving you Rising Star, Miss Armstrong. I've never seen her perform that way. She deserves to be yours."

"But she's a valuable animal!"

The earl looked quizzical. "I've lost valuable animals in card games, my dear. Much better to see that one is owned by someone who will recognize and elicit her true potential. If she stayed here at Combe Park, we would be constantly plagued by her misbehavior, and if someone else owned her, I could not be certain of her treatment."

"You are exceedingly kind, but I could not possibly accept her," Nell protested.

"Why ever not?" Lord Westwick hooked his arm with hers and motioned for Sir Hugh to follow them. "I've arranged for tea in the gold parlor, since we're all in our riding clothes. My wife always insisted on that, and I've continued the policy. When you get to be my age, it's not so easy to break long-standing habits. But you're young, my dear, and needn't cling to useless principles and wasteful proprieties."

"In addition to those useless principles and wasteful proprieties," Nell insisted, "there is the small matter of my being quite unable to afford a horse in Bath. At Longstreet Manor I might perhaps overcome my principles enough to add one more mouth to the small selection of horses we possess, but that is scarcely the case here."

"Of course it isn't," the earl agreed cheerfully. "You won't have to take care of her in Bath, Miss Armstrong. I shall simply have her moved to my stable there, where she will stay, ready for your use at any time, until you remove to Westmorland once again."

"Or she might join my horses," Sir Hugh suggested. "Another mouth won't be noticed there, and I think perhaps it would be easier for Miss Armstrong to explain riding a horse from my stable than one from yours, sir."

"Ah, yes. Miss Longstreet's aversion to me might cramp Miss Armstrong's ability to ride when she pleased, might it not? A very good suggestion, Sir Hugh."

"No, it is not," Nell protested. "I could no more accept such a favor from Sir Hugh than I could such an extravagant gift from Lord Westwick."

"Perhaps she's right, Westwick. Rising Star had best stay with Emily and John's horses. There could be no whiff of impropriety about that."

Lord Westwick hesitated slightly, looking a little concerned, but eventually he nodded. "Very well, with the Holmslys' horses, then."

Nell, who was apparently not to be consulted about this matter, allowed herself to be ushered into the gold parlor. It was a bright but casual room with shining parquet floors and mullioned windows. The tea tray had already been set out, along with a large silver plate of tempting delicacies. Nell was asked by the earl to pour their tea, which she did with her usual efficiency. By the time she was able to sit back and take a sip of her own tea, the discussion had moved on to other matters. Though she was too polite to interrupt, she had by no means accepted the men's pronouncements on what was to become of Rising Star.

Sir Hugh was querying the earl on how he managed his seat in Westmorland when he never went there. "I get urgent missives from my estate agent whenever I'm away for more than three days," he protested. "You say you've scarcely been to Westmorland in forty years!"

"When it became clear that my wife and I weren't going to have any children, I turned the place over to my presumptive heir, with the understanding that if that situation changed to his disadvantage, I would procure a similar property for him. It wasn't a perfect solution, but it has served very well." The earl set his teacup on a small table and helped himself to a treacle biscuit. "For many years he has been secure in the knowledge that it will legally be his property, and he has been an excellent steward."

Nell wanted very much to ask him why he had never returned to Westmorland. Surely being rejected by his fiancée could not have been so distressing that he would give up his own home. "Did Lady Westwick not care for the Westmorland countryside?" she finally asked.

"We both preferred Bath," he replied with a decided finality. Then he smiled at his guests. "But I could not resist Combe Park when it came up for sale thirty-odd years ago. Horses have always been a passion with me. My wife understood that, and was more than agreeable about this place."

"Everything about it is exceptional," Nell said. "A truly delightful setting, a charming house, and such a thriving stable. Which, I might add, is not going to lose Rising Star on my behalf."

"Ah, we shall see," the earl replied, shaking a playful finger at her. "At least for the time being, you will allow me to make her available to you in Bath, as a favor to an aging fellow who would get great pleasure from the service."

This offer Nell could not refuse, and so she graciously accepted, saying, "You are too good to me, Lord Westwick. It will be entirely my pleasure to ride her."

Sir Hugh took it upon himself to arrange for Rising Star to be accommodated in his brother-in-law's stables. His sister was delighted, but wondered aloud, "You don't think Lord Westwick is smitten with her, do you? Dear Nell must be more than thirty years younger than he is!"

"No, it is merely a kindness, Emily. The poor man is still grieving for his wife, for heaven's sake."

"Yes, so I thought. But Nell might very easily turn a man's head, you know. She has that rare combination of countenance, good humor, and practicality, to say nothing of a touch of feyness."

"Feyness?"

Emily nodded thoughtfully. "There's something dreamy about her. An odd kick to her gallop, as Papa used to say. I like it."

Hugh liked it, too, but he was not going to advise his sister of that fact. "You like her because she finds you charming," he teased.

His sister laughed. "Well, there is that. And she likes little Walter. Which is a great deal more than one can say for her aunt!"

"Yes, indeed. Have you by any chance met my godmother's friend Mrs. Dorsey?"

"I'm quite sure Miss Longstreet has no friends, Hugh."

Her brother grinned. "Well, this is an old and long-standing acquaintance, I believe, formed in girlhood during their London Season."

"It's hard to believe that Miss Longstreet was ever a girl," Emily mused. "And, no, I haven't met a Mrs. Dorsey. Why do you ask?"

Hugh considered how much would be wise to divulge to his curious sister. "There's something havey-cavey going on with Miss Longstreet, and it has a connection to Mrs. Dorsey, though she seems a perfectly pleasant and decent sort of woman."

"Unlike your godmother," muttered Emily as she set a stitch in her embroidery.

"Quite. But Miss Armstrong is concerned that her aunt is plotting some mischief."

Emily's head came up sharply from her work. "Since when has Nell taken to confiding such things in you? She has told me nothing of this."

"Perhaps that is because of your penchant for rushing in to solve everyone else's problems, my dear sister. I believe Miss Armstrong—Nell—does not wish to precipitate any action on her aunt's part by confronting her with her suspicions."

"As though I would confront that old harridan! She would tell me to mind my own business, or worse!"

"Precisely. Nell," he said, enjoying the sound of her name on his tongue, "told me on our drive back from Combe Park that Mrs. Dorsey had mentioned in passing that Miss Longstreet had once been engaged to marry Lord Westwick."

"Never!" Emily looked truly appalled. "I cannot believe that even as a young man the earl could have been so lacking in judgment. And why would she have turned him off? Answer me that."

"I cannot. It is possible, I suppose, that Mrs. Dorsey is mistaken. But somehow I doubt it. What Nell wondered, and I can see her point in this, is whether any of Mama's old correspondence with Miss Longstreet might have survived. It was the three of them—Mama, Miss Longstreet, and Mrs. Dorsey—who were such bosom beaux at the time. If indeed Miss Longstreet was engaged to Lord Westwick, it would surely have been discussed in their letters, along with the reasons for the termination of the engagement."

Emily's brow wrinkled in concentration. "Mama did save her correspondence with a few people. I have no idea whether Miss Longstreet was one of them, though it would seem likely since she was your godmama. When Mama died . . . I don't know, Hugh. Perhaps the letters were destroyed. Or they might have been relegated to the attics. It is years ago, and I was not fully grown. The Fallings housekeeper at the time is likely the one who would know, but she has retired, has she not?"

"Three years ago. I could write to her, but her memory was failing when she left. It might be simpler to have Mrs. Luther make a search of the attics."

"Do," Emily urged. "I would give a great deal to know the whole of this story."

"So would I."

Chapter Twelve

Though Nell had attempted to query her aunt about Mrs. Dorsey's visit, the stubborn woman would say nothing more than "She's gotten quite old." No use pointing out that Mrs. Dorsey was no older than Aunt Longstreet, of course.

A few days after her visit to Combe Park, Nell set down her cup of chocolate at the breakfast table and regarded her companion with curiosity. "Don't you wish to pay Mrs. Dorsey a call, Aunt? I'm sure she would love for you to see her house. The whole of it is like a conservatory, there are so many plants. Shall I arrange to take you there this afternoon?"

"I'm perfectly capable of arranging to get myself anywhere I wish," Rosemarie grumbled. "In fact, I may very well decide to visit Gertrude this afternoon, but I shall do so on my own. Surely you can find something more interesting to do in Bath than visit with two old ladies."

"Well, if you won't be needing me, I believe I shall go riding with Emily Holmsly later on."

"You would do better to make friends with more serious ladies, Helen. Mrs. Holmsly is no more than a social gadabout."

"I'm fond of her. And I long for a ride."

"You can ride in the country. Here in town you might pursue more sophisticated interests. Go to a museum, visit an art exhibit, study the architecture."

"Ah, but I might develop a taste for that kind of amusement," Nell teased, "and what would I do when we are back in the country?"

"No one is keeping you from pursuing such interests in the country," her aunt sniffed.

Nell smiled only slightly when she said, "No, indeed, ma'am."

"Humpf!"

And so Nell rode out with Emily, and Lord Westwick, and Sir Hugh. If she felt guilty about deceiving her aunt, the emotion was only fleeting once she was astride Rising Star. The immediate rapport she had felt with the mare only seemed to grow stronger as the days passed. The earl was unfailingly kind to her, almost as though she were a favorite relation of his. Nell knew he was lonely and felt gratified that she and Emily seemed to amuse him. So it was with a great deal of surprise that she heard Emily comment to her brother one day as they walked back from the stables after the earl had left them, "I think Lord Westwick is taken with our Nell, don't you?"

Sir Hugh looked as surprised, and distressed, as Nell felt. "Good lord, Emily, the man is old enough to be her grandfather! You shouldn't be putting such notions in Miss Armstrong's head!"

Nell did not like it that the baronet thought she would for a moment contemplate such a "notion," and she said stiffly, "I assure you it is the farthest thing from my mind. If I suspected that Lord Westwick thought of me as anything other than a young friend, I would be unable to accept the loan of his horse for so much as a ride."

Emily colored with chagrin. "You quite mistake me, Hugh! That is not at all what I meant. Gracious, his lordship is hardly on the lookout for a young wife! He was so entirely devoted to Lady Westwick that I daresay he wouldn't even think of marrying again."

Sir Hugh halted in the path, offering her a stiff bow. "I beg your pardon. I seem to have misunderstood you, and in turn to have been misunderstood by Miss Armstrong. It was not my intention to distress either of you. I spoke entirely out of turn, and I pray you will both disregard my careless words."

Although Nell attempted to graciously accept his apology, she found that in fact she could not. It seemed to her that Sir Hugh had just suggested that she was someone who would encourage the attentions of a lonely old man, making a push to get an offer of marriage from him. She had thought Sir Hugh had a better opinion of her. She had *hoped* Sir Hugh had a better opinion of her. Ordinarily he walked with her from Emily's house to Queen Square, but on this occasion Nell told him she would be going to the library and really did not need his escort.

"My dear Miss Armstrong," he protested, "I would be pleased to walk with you to the library."

"Thank you, but I feel certain you have other things to do."

"Nothing I would prefer to accompanying you." Sir Hugh frowned and cocked his head at her. "You're angry with me, aren't you?"

"Of course not! How should I be? I merely feel that I have taken up enough of your time today."

"Well, you haven't," he said frankly. "If you can think of a better excuse, I shall consider it. Come, the library is on my route, and you and I have matters to discuss."

Nell reluctantly allowed him to place her hand on his arm. "Such as?" she asked stiffly.

"I should very much like to know if you've learned anything more about your aunt's relationship with Lord Westwick. And I wished to let you know that I've sent off an express to the housekeeper at Fallings with the request that she search for any of my mother's letters that may have survived."

"Is she likely to find any?"

"That's hard to say. Your aunt is my godmother, of course, so it is quite possible that my mother saved her letters. Whether they still exist . . ." He shrugged. "Tell me what you've learned."

"Almost nothing," she admitted. "My aunt has visited Mrs. Dorsey, and vice versa, but is not in the least forthcoming about their time together or their original friendship."

"Does Miss Longstreet say anything about Lord West-wick?"

Nell shook her head. "Not recently. She decreed that I was to have nothing to do with him, but I told her that would be impossible if she were unable to explain why not."

Sir Hugh shook his head with amusement. "And you appear such an accommodating young lady."

"I am, but I will not be imposed upon," she said, remembering that she was displeased with the baronet. "I have not told her about Rising Star, which is no doubt very wrong of me."

"It would merely distress her, and it is none of her business."

"That is the rationalization I use, certainly, but there is the matter of loyalty."

Sir Hugh did not reply to this, and they walked on in silence. When they reached the library, Sir Hugh said, "I would be happy to wait for you, Miss Armstrong."

"No, no. I will be some time and refuse to delay you further, sir."

"As you wish. Is this a day when Mr. Bentley is working?"

"I have no idea."

Sir Hugh bowed and turned away. Nell watched as he strolled casually down the street, nodding to acquaintances and stopping to speak with a very pretty young lady. With a sigh Nell hurried into the library.

*   *   *

Sir Hugh had been caught off guard by his sister's remark. He had been thinking how well Nell rode Rising Star, and how thoughtful it was of Lord Westwick to provide a mount for the young woman. Perhaps there was that questioning in his mind about the motivation for this latter action which made him jump to the conclusion that his sister was hinting at a match between the elderly lord and the impecunious Miss Armstrong. It was the sort of thing Emily loved to promote—the solution to two people's problems in one fell swoop.

The very idea had appalled him. Surely one always shuddered at the thought of a young woman with a man so much older. It seemed quite unfair, if not a little obscene. Sir Hugh was immensely fond of Lord Westwick, and considered him a vigorous, charming man. But as a husband for Miss Armstrong! No, indeed.

And even though Emily had denied such a thought, and Nell had spurned it, Sir Hugh could not get the idea out of his head once it had lodged there. What if Lord Westwick, lonely and heirless as he was, had conceived of just such a plan? Surely it had been extraordinarily generous of him to offer so valuable a horse to a young lady he scarcely knew. And Nell had that delightful combination of wistfulness and capability that would just suit a man of Westwick's years, wouldn't it? She was not at all like Lady Westwick, and therefore could not compete in that field, but she was a unique and winsome thing that might seem perfectly acceptable to the earl in his partnerless state. Giving her the horse provided the perfect opportunity for him to see her nearly every day, when the party of four rode out together.

Though Sir Hugh attempted to dissuade himself of this scenario, he was not entirely successful. On the following days he observed the earl keenly in his dealings with Miss Armstrong, and every day there was a new invitation to try to dismiss from his mind. Lord Westwick had Nell—and the rest of the party—to tea at his house on the Parade. He suggested a musical evening—which Sir Hugh knew that Nell would not be able to refuse. He invited Nell and Emily to his house so that Nell might try out the exquisite pianoforte that his wife had played. He even tried to get Nell to accept a pair of fine leather riding gloves that "were just lying about Combe Park." As though he hadn't purchased them for her himself! Hugh could see that they were as unused as a new minted penny.

Nell modestly protested such largesse, but Emily was always there to convince her of the acceptability of it. "Now, what is the sense in refusing a pair of gloves which aren't being used by anyone else?" she demanded. "Don't be such a nodcock." No one mentioned, though it was more than obvious, that Nell's own gloves were worn and beginning to fray.

Hugh was determined to learn the truth of the matter. Was the Earl of Westwick courting Miss Armstrong, or was he not? Though he knew himself to have no right to ask, Hugh was determined to learn the answer to this irritating question. And so one day he took himself off to the earl's house, where he planned to confront the man. He went unannounced so as to give his lordship no chance to prepare an evasive answer.

His first surprise was in being kept waiting. The earl, apparently, was with his man of business on an important matter and would be with the baronet as soon as possible. Hugh cooled his heels in the charming sunny room with its sparkling crystals and bright fabrics. He was not uplifted by the decor on this occasion, but rather annoyed by the thought that Nell would undoubtedly adore the room—when she came to the house on the Parade as its mistress.

His next discovery was how awkward an interview this was likely to prove. When the earl entered the room, smiling and apologizing for keeping Hugh waiting, the baronet had not the least idea how to approach the subject without sounding like a fool. When Lord Westwick expressed his pleasure at seeing Hugh and asked if there was anything in particular that he could do for the younger man, Hugh floundered, "Well, sir, I . . ."

"Seems to me," Lord Westwick said, waving him to a chair, "that it's time you called me Carstairs. It's a wretched mouthful as a given name, I know, but it's all my own. My dearly beloved wife could never quite bring herself to use it and called me Westwick our entire married life." He gave a soft laugh. "I should like to think I have a few friends who are brave enough to attempt it."

"Certainly . . . Carstairs." Now, what was he supposed to say? "And I trust you will feel perfectly comfortable calling me Hugh, as almost everyone does."

"Not Miss Armstrong, I've noticed," the earl remarked with a ruminative air. "Considering her friendship with your sister and yourself, that surprises me a little."

Hugh was trying to remember if the earl called Nell by her given name, but could not believe that he did. "Miss Armstrong has not given me explicit permission to use her name. I've heard her aunt call her Helen, but of course my sister calls her Nell."

"Charming name, Nell. And Helen as well, though it has a more formal, solid sound than Nell, don't you think?"

"I do."

"And yet they both suit her, Nell and Helen. She's quite an original combination of naïveté and knowledge." Suddenly the earl regarded him keenly. "I fear you will consider me impertinent, Hugh, but I must ask you this. My understanding—and that of society at large—is that you are to inherit Miss Longstreet's property in Westmorland. Do you know if she has made any provision for Miss Armstrong?"

Hugh's posture stiffened, and it was some little time before he answered. The only thing which convinced him to reply at all was the realization that he had been about to tax the earl with something just as little his business as was this of the earl's. "It has been my understanding since I was a child that my godmother had intended to make me her heir. However, she has come to take me in some dislike, I believe, and it seems more than likely to me that she will make Miss Armstrong her heir."

The earl shook his head. "Unlikely. Rosemarie has a sense of tradition which would forbid her bequeathing a whole estate to a possibly illegitimate niece. No, no, don't scowl at me that way. I'm aware of the likelihood that Margaret married her swain. I may not have spent much time in Westmorland, but early on I had plenty of people willing to send me the county gossip."

"Then you will know that Miss Armstrong has been with her aunt for ten years and makes her home at Longstreet Manor. She does not believe that her aunt intends to leave her the property, or even to make any significant provision for her. I personally find that difficult to accept."

"Difficult, yes, but not impossible." The earl sat for some time with his head bent, thinking. As though he at length had made up his mind, he raised his head and regarded Hugh solemnly. "I intend to make provision for Miss Armstrong. Her situation is untenable, and I am in a position to right it."

Hugh was stunned. "You intend to marry her?"

"Marry her?" The earl frowned. "No, of course not. Why would she wish to marry an old goat like me?"

"Begging your pardon, sir, you are hardly an old goat. And you would be making her the Countess of Westwick."

The earl shook his head. "Miss Armstrong has much too good sense to marry for a title. No, I've been trying to settle on a plan with my man of business. It is all very well to leave her my unentailed property at my death, but what is she to do in the meantime? She must have a decent allowance if she is to remain with her aunt, and a real inheritance if she is to leave her."

Hugh's mind reeled. "But why? Excuse me for saying so, sir, but you haven't the right to provide for Miss Armstrong. Imagine the gossip if you were to do anything on that order. People would be vicious in their assumptions."

"What people?" the earl demanded. "Would any of these people be someone whom Miss Armstrong knew or cared about? Would you or your sister make such assumptions?"

"Of course not! But you know our society. They'd eat her alive."

The earl winced. "Dammit! That's why I can't figure out how to do it, Hugh. If Rosemarie and I were on decent terms, I'd arrange it with her. But she would more likely spit on me than agree to help her niece."

"And why is that, sir?"

The earl sighed but shook his head. "I would rather not go into that. Let me just say that there seems no chance of changing that situation. But I refuse to allow Miss Armstrong to languish as an impoverished country miss for lack of funds. Greenlaw, my man of business, suggests an anonymous trust set up to provide for her, but I can't see that that would be any more acceptable to the gossips. Plus, it would mean that trustees would have a certain measure of control. And she really needs an allowance now."

"Her aunt should provide her a decent allowance," Hugh protested. "Did she wear that lovely emerald gown when you took her to the concert?"

The earl's eyes danced. "She did. What a charmer she looked, but I swear the dress must have wiped her out for the quarter. She confessed that Madame de Vigne made it and that there was not enough left over for matching shoes."

Nell hadn't told him that, Hugh thought wistfully. It certainly spoke to her feeling completely comfortable with the earl, in a way she did not feel with him. But it might also signify that she thought of this older man as a suitor. "You don't think that perhaps Miss Armstrong will perceive your many attentions toward her as being those of a suitor?" he asked diffidently.

"No, my boy, I do not. I am the soul of avuncular bonhomie when I am with her, am I not?"

"So it would seem to you and me, but perhaps to an inexperienced girl such as Miss Armstrong . . ."

"Inexperienced perhaps, but not lacking in intelligence. Miss Armstrong will not confuse my intentions."

"But surely others might."

"Hugh, my dear fellow, you worry too much. Are you and your sister not there on almost every occasion when I am in Miss Armstrong's company? She would as like misconstrue your constant presence."

Having delivered himself of this home truth, the earl winked at his guest and changed the subject. Hugh left shortly thereafter, only slightly more disconcerted than he had been before he arrived.

Chapter Thirteen

Emily had little difficulty convincing Nell to join Mrs.
Gorton's young set to learn country-dances after Rosemarie Longstreet made her announcement that they would
attend another assembly. This change of heart had astonished Nell, especially when her aunt continued, "We shall
take Mrs. Dorsey, and you may invite Sir Hugh to escort
us," she said grudgingly. "A week Thursday, if you please.
That will give us plenty of time."

Plenty of time for what? Nell wondered, but she knew it
was useless to inquire of her secretive aunt. What it would
give *her* time for, she hoped, was a foray into the art of
country-dancing, under Emily's auspices. Emily first offered private instruction in the parlor of the house in Queen
Square, where Rosemarie was disposed to observe and criticize. "Gracefully, gracefully! Above all you must have a
lightness to your step! And a smile on your face, missy, not
that look of abject concentration. See how Mrs. Holmsly's
eyes sparkle as she whirls."

Emily giggled, it being a new experience for her to have
the fault-finding lady approve of her behavior in any way.
"It's called flirting," she whispered to Nell. "The gentlemen
expect it."

"Perhaps that is because you are a married woman. I cannot think it proper for me to flirt with a dancing partner."

"Oh, indeed it is. You must look him in the eye the whole

time you're dancing, and let him know how utterly fascinating you find him."

"Ah, you wish me to deceive."

"Tsk! How can you say such a thing? You will be dancing with Hugh and with Lord Westwick, and they are both perfectly fascinating gentlemen."

"Lord Westwick?" Rosemarie demanded. "Why would you be dancing with Lord Westwick, Helen?"

The young ladies had been careful to keep the earl out of their conversation, and it was a slip on Emily's part to mention him. So far as Aunt Longstreet knew, all Nell's adventures had been in the company of Emily and/or her brother.

"Lord Westwick is a particular friend of mine," Emily recovered now, "and he will most assuredly wish to dance with my dear friend Nell."

Nell was very much afraid that her aunt would have something to say about this, but her aunt, uncharacteristically, restrained herself. With one of her accustomed *humpf*'s she turned and left the room. Nell sighed her relief.

"I'm very sorry for mentioning the earl," Emily apologized when they were alone. "It is so terribly difficult to remember that Miss Longstreet was once engaged to him. It seems so unlikely! Have you not found out more about it?"

Nell shook her head. "She's so adamant on the subject of his lordship that I daren't even mention his name. Come, show me which hand I offer for the crossover."

Nell was surprised, and not quite pleased, to find that Emily had invited Sir Hugh to join them for the dancing lessons. "The more the merrier!" Mrs. Gorton assured Sir Hugh, her face beaming. "My daughters will be enchanted to have a man of your address, and my sons will plague you about their driving skills. If you are brave enough to face them all, I'm more than happy to have you."

Nell noted that the baronet was indeed a patient parti,

joining in the lessons as though he took pleasure in instructing the youngsters in the intricacies of country-dances. He was an elegant dancer himself, and the schoolroom party sought to emulate him, but they were young and their spirits were high. His toes were trod upon with giddy apologies, and his attention plucked at every break in the music for his young admirers to query him on the finer points of boxing or driving. Sir Hugh was good-humored through it all.

And Nell began to understand her own part as he partnered her through dance after dance, explaining the steps. "Of course that would not be allowed at an assembly," Emily admitted when the party at length broke up, "but here it does not matter in the least. At the Lower Rooms you may stand up for no more than two sets with any given gentleman during the whole of the evening."

Nell laughed. "I shall be astonished if any gentleman wishes to dance a second set with me once he has seen how prone I am to going in the wrong direction."

"You did remarkably well," Sir Hugh assured her with a smile. "And if my toes are recovered by the next assembly, I beg you will stand up with me for the first and last sets."

"You are too kind, Sir Hugh," she replied with a mock curtsy before proceeding along the street with her two companions.

"Not at all. I'm gratified that my godmother has requested my escort. Astonished, but gratified."

"I must admit that I was a little taken aback myself, but that is not my greatest concern. I very much fear that whatever Aunt Longstreet is planning to do, it will happen at the Lower Rooms. We're to take Mrs. Dorsey with us, and though I cannot see her as an accomplice to anything wicked, she may prove an inadvertent witness for my aunt."

Hugh's brows lowered, and he gave a tsk of annoyance. "I wish I had heard back from my housekeeper. I am in daily expectation of some word. I'll contact you directly I hear anything of interest."

Emily clapped her hands with excitement. "Oh, I can scarcely wait! Knowing your aunt, Nell, I am sure she intends to set Bath by its ear. And she has already given Lord Westwick the cut direct. What can she possibly have in mind to follow up on that?"

"Emily," her brother said sternly, "this is not a matter of amusement for Miss Armstrong. How would you feel if your husband created a scandal at the Lower Rooms? It would be a matter of acute embarrassment."

"Yes, but John *wouldn't* create a scandal, which everyone knows. And those who know Miss Longstreet will not be at all surprised to have her do something outrageous, will they?"

"They may not be surprised, but that won't lessen Miss Armstrong's discomfort, will it?"

Nell, unwilling to take part in their discussion, watched the brother and sister from under the brim of her bonnet, trying to decipher if either was likely to take her in disgust if her aunt's behavior should be especially bad. Emily put a protective arm about her waist, saying, "Well, if Miss Longstreet goes beyond the pale, I tell you what I have in mind, Hugh. Nell must come to live with me. There, I knew it would shock you both, but I've given it a great deal of thought. We get along famously, and I am a great deal easier to live with than your impossible godmother. Living with me, too, Nell would have a chance to meet some worthy gentleman who does not require a handsome bridal portion. And do not tell me there are no men of that caliber, because I know there are!"

"Oh, no, no, no, no, no!" Nell had paled and could not seem to stop shaking her head. "It is very good of you, Emily, but most unnecessary. Aunt Longstreet is my family, Longstreet Manor is my home. And even if she should do something so awful that I cannot raise my head in Bath, well, we will soon be back in Westmorland, where no one will know anything of the matter."

Sir Hugh looked so alarmed by Emily's suggestion that he could scarcely decide where to begin with his objections. In the gap before he could begin his list of reasons why hers was an impossible idea, Emily herself straightened to her full height. "My dear Nell, family is supposed to protect you and to care for you. Your aunt has no intention of carrying out either of those responsibilities. Ergo, she is scarcely family at all, and certainly you would be well rid of her!"

"As usual, my dear Emily, your reasoning is impeccable," her brother informed her with exasperation. "I have no doubt that it is your warm heart and earnest sense of justice which have led you to make so generous an offer, but you must see, as Miss Armstrong does, that it will not do!"

"No," Emily stoutly replied, "I do not see that at all."

"Have you, for instance, mentioned your plan to your husband?" Hugh asked.

"Not yet, but I have every reason to believe that he will be as enamored of the idea as I am myself. Does he not disappear every other day and expect me to amuse myself without him? He does indeed. It would be of great benefit to him, and to me, to have company during his long and inexplicable absences, would it not? Yes, it would."

She could have gone on in this vein for some time, but fortunately they were passing the library, and who should appear before them but Mr. Bentley. Nell had scarcely ever been so glad to see anyone.

"Why, Miss Armstrong and Mrs. Holmsly! How do you do? What good fortune that I should have encountered you, for I have but only received the latest book from the author of *Mansfield Park*, and I knew you would wish to be advised of the circumstance. I have," he admitted with a pleased conspiratorial grin, "put it aside for you."

"Mr. Bentley! How kind! Are you acquainted with Sir Hugh Nowlin? He is Mrs. Holmsly's brother."

The two men bowed and, to Nell's eyes, appeared to take skeptical assessment of one another. Nell remembered that Sir Hugh had threatened—well, offered—to have Mr. Bentley's credentials checked, and she watched his face nervously. But he was all politeness to the librarian, thanking Mr. Bentley for his services to his godmother and his companions.

"It is my pleasure," the young man assured him. "Shall I just run in and get the book for you, Miss Armstrong?"

"No, why don't I come with you? There is something I . . . And I can make my own way home, Emily and Sir Hugh. Thank you so much for the lessons."

Without checking to see what their reaction was to this cowardly withdrawal, she hastened into the library, with Mr. Bentley scurrying to catch up and assuring her, "I can see you home myself, Miss Armstrong. I was just leaving."

Sir Hugh made no progress in convincing his sister that her plan was ineligible. For every argument he put forth, she came up with a new—and to her more brilliant—one. "And, Hugh, imagine! She will be able to wear all of my dresses."

"Not unless she shrinks three inches."

"Pish! A row of trimming at the hem—it is of no consequence. Oh, I shall love dressing her. She's so attractive when she wears that green gown."

"She's attractive when she wears her old-fashioned gowns, Emily."

"Yes, but the old quizzes make fun of them. You know they do, Hugh. It would be so much better for her to have something fashionable. And I shall ask Catherine to send me any of her gowns that she is finished with, for I'm sure she is a good two inches taller than I."

"It won't do, Emily," Hugh said firmly as they neared her

house. "Miss Armstrong is a proud woman; she would not be willing to accept charity from you."

"But she would be my companion!"

"She is already Miss Longstreet's companion, and it is a more fitting, if less comfortable, position than living with you."

"But I cannot bear to think of her going back to Westmorland and living in some isolated country house with that cross old lady!" Tears welled in his sister's eyes, and she reached an imploring hand out to him. "Hugh, we must do something for her. Can't you see that?"

He squeezed her fingers and smiled gently down at her. "You've done something already, Emily, by being her friend. I think it was Nell's lucky day when she came to Bath."

Which was all he felt able to tell her. Lord Westwick had not given him permission to even hint at any financial aid he might offer the young lady. And Hugh still felt rather torn as to whether he approved of that solution.

"Oh, yes, I think it was. For no one knew of her plight before this. Do you think perhaps Mr. Bentley will come into a sudden inheritance and be able to marry her?"

"No, I do not!"

"Perhaps he is independently wealthy and only enjoys working at the library."

"I should think it most unlikely."

Emily sighed as she paused at her front door. "We'll find a way to help, won't we, Hugh?"

"Yes, my dear. We'll find a way."

Hugh watched her disappear into her house. *We* will find a way did not quite satisfy his feelings on the subject. Both Emily and Lord Westwick were determined to help Nell Armstrong out of a situation that they felt intolerable. Hugh was less concerned with the situation itself than with the young lady who gave rise to their concerns.

His delightful daily contact with her, his irritation with the perfectly unexceptionable librarian, and his distress at Westwick's and Emily's proposals suggested that he should do a little soul-searching about his own feelings toward Nell. Unfortunately, he never got far before he was brought up sharply by the realization that anything he felt might be tainted by their positions as rival heirs for Miss Longstreet's property.

Yes, he anticipated their afternoon rides together. Indeed, when she smiled that conspiratorial smile at him, as though the two of them had some special understanding of the world, he felt so warmed that he longed to hug her to his chest. Perhaps, even, he felt more elementary stirrings when she placed her hand on his arm, when her trusting eyes sought out his own.

And there had been a few dreams . . . Well, the less said on that head, the better. She was a properly brought-up young lady, not a lightskirt. But he had known in those dreams that she was a sensuous woman, not the least bit a prude. A dream lover who . . .

Hugh shook his head and proceeded on down the Circus toward his own apartments. The reality of the situation was that she considered herself bound to remain with her aunt, and she would certainly wonder at any signs of attention from him, knowing that he believed she might inherit Miss Longstreet's property. Because she did not in her naïveté realize how unique she was, she could scarcely attribute honorable motives to his interest.

Nor had she had the opportunity to meet a sufficient number and variety of gentlemen to find one in whom she might be interested. If he were to attempt to win her regard, wouldn't he be seen as taking unfair advantage of her? Not that the opinion of others was so important, but would it not be the truth? And there was, again, that self-interest which might actually be influencing him as well.

This had become the usual tangle of his thoughts on the subject of Nell Armstrong, and it was almost with relief that he spied his friend Hopkins approaching from the opposite direction.

"Hugh! Haven't seen you in days, dear fellow. Something up?"

"Dancing attendance upon my sister and her friend," Hugh admitted. "Holmsly seems to be gone a good deal, and Emily frets."

"I should be very happy to keep her company," Hopkins offered. "' Course, I heard she slapped some poor fellow who visited."

"Who tried to kiss her, more like," Hugh muttered. "My sister's good spirits are occasionally misunderstood by the local rakehells."

"Well, you know you can trust me not to cross the line, my good fellow. What ails Holmsly that he don't spend more time with his bride?"

"Business matters, I gather."

Hopkins pursed his lips. "Hmm. Thought I saw him 'tother day, you know, south of Bath. But he must not have recognized me, as he rode off without a word."

Hugh's gaze sharpened. "South of Bath? Anywhere near Combe Park?"

"Not far, now you mention it. We were returning from Prior Park. Lovely place."

Hugh didn't tell him that Holmsly's business was ostensibly in Bristol, not at all in the direction of Prior Park, or Combe Park, for that matter. But it certainly gave him a moment's pause, since Nell, too, had thought she'd seen his brother-in-law in that area. To Hopkins he said, "Why not call on Emily now? Ask her about the dancing lessons."

"Dancing lessons, eh? Ain't had dancing lessons since I was in short pants."

A pure fabrication, of course, and Hugh laughed. "I'm not

surprised you were a dancing prodigy, Horace. Go see Emily; she will press you into service."

"Happy to oblige her in any way," Hopkins assured him, as he tipped his hat in farewell.

One more mystery to unravel, Hugh mused as he strolled on down the street. He had been willing to believe that Nell could have misidentified John Holmsly in the country. She scarcely knew him. But Hopkins had known Holmsly most of his life, and if he said he'd seen him near Combe Park, then that's where Holmsly had been. But why had he been there—when he was supposed to be in Bristol on business?

Hugh very much feared he did not want to know the answer to that question, nor to have Emily know it.

But the matter of his brother-in-law's whereabouts completely disappeared from his mind when he found the packet of his mother's letters on the salver in the hall. Mrs. Luther had finally been successful in her search.

Chapter Fourteen

Nell was a little alarmed to receive a call from Sir Hugh that afternoon. Her aunt was out visiting Mrs. Dorsey, so Nell would have to welcome him on her own. Though she had appreciated his defense of her position to his sister, she certainly did not wish to discuss the matter further. And it occurred to her that he might think she had induced Emily to make that suggestion that she be her permanent companion. Therefore, her smile was hesitant when Sir Hugh was ushered into the parlor by Woodbridge.

His first words surprised her: "Miss Armstrong, may I call you Nell?"

"But of course. Your sister has been calling me Nell since we met."

"I know, and it is very awkward to be forever addressing you as Miss Armstrong when in the next breath Emily is saying Nell this and Nell that."

"I do prefer Nell to Helen, however. Only my aunt calls me Helen."

"So I've noticed." He placed a packet of letters on the table as he seated himself across from her. "I trust your aunt has gone out? These arrived today from my housekeeper. I think they answer our questions about Miss Longstreet and Lord Westwick."

He sounded so serious that Nell clutched her hands tightly

in her lap. "Yes, my aunt should be gone for some time. What do the letters say?"

"You should read the pertinent ones," he said, reaching to lift the first one from the stack. "We have only my godmother's word for what happened, of course, but I see no reason to disbelieve her, as these letters were written at the time of the events."

Nell accepted the first missive with slightly trembling fingers. It was dated more than forty years in the past and began with the salutation "My dear Amelia." She immediately recognized her aunt's impressive copperplate handwriting, large and self-assured as it was. There were a few lines congratulating Lady Nowlin on her state of impending motherhood before Rosemarie Longstreet launched into her own news:

> *I must tell you that the long-awaited proposal has been made and accepted. Carstairs Tollson applied to my father last week for the right to pay his addresses to me. It was prettily done, as one would expect. He is such a handsome fellow, as you will remember from meeting him in London, and his being almost a neighbor is such a fortunate thing.*
>
> *We have set no date as yet. Mama seems to think there is no sense rushing into what will carry me away from the Manor, when I bring a "calming" influence on my sister Margaret. I am not impatient to be off myself, as I understand old Lord Westwick has been ill for some time, and we will be forced to live in his household for the time being. But I believe the earl has expressed a wish to see Carstairs married before he passes on. Not that this is imminently expected. I trust our nuptials will take place in a few months.*

Nell looked up from the letter to say, "There is a lack of excitement about her acceptance, isn't there? It sounds almost as though it were an arranged marriage."

"Well, they would have known each other, and it would

have been a beneficial alliance on both sides, I daresay. Read your aunt's next letter to my mother."

This one was dated three months later. The pertinent information was offered in a slightly irritated tone:

> *The old lord has died. Though he had been sickly for some time, no one expected his death. I must say it is very aggravating. Now we are supposed to wait out the year of mourning before we marry. I cannot believe it is necessary, but apparently Carstairs' mother insists that it would be disrespectful to her husband's memory if we were not to adhere to this antiquated custom. I cannot see how! Her husband wished for our marriage before his death and would no doubt be annoyed by its delay, but no one pays any attention to my opinion on the matter. Both my parents agree that it is Lady Westwick's right to demand this of her son and his bride.*

Without saying anything, Hugh handed her the third letter. This one was dated six months after its predecessor.

> *You will not credit what has happened, Amelia! I can scarce believe it myself. This morning I received a call from Carstairs. It had been almost a month since we had last seen him. He sought an interview with my father first, and Mama and I could hear father's voice bellowing all the way down the hall, though we could not distinguish the words. Mama was quite alarmed. She suggested that I go above to my chamber, but I am not so chicken-hearted!*
>
> *When Papa came from his study, he was red in the face and would say nothing but "Out!" to the new earl. Carstairs hesitated, saying, "I really should speak to Miss Longstreet, sir." But Papa would have none of it. He kept mumbling things like "miscreant," "cad," and the like. Some of the terms I was not even familiar with! But you may be sure that Mama and I got the idea that the earl was no longer welcome in our house.*
>
> *With a stiff bow, Carstairs left. Papa was so distressed that he was unable to speak. Mama insisted that he sit*

down, and while she was ministering to him I slipped out of the room and ran after Carstairs. I caught up with him just short of the stables. When he heard me, he stopped and waited for me. His face was quite white, whether with anger or some other emotion I was unable to tell. He held his hands out to me and clasped mine so tightly that they hurt. "Miss Longstreet! Thank you for coming. I have done you a dreadful wrong, and I would have been even more distressed to leave without telling you to your face."

Even then I did not comprehend of what he spoke. Well, who would have? I had always considered him a man of honor, as did we all. Otherwise I would not have agreed to ally myself with him. So what he had to say not only stunned but disgusted me, and I pulled my hands from his in real horror.

How could he so humiliate me? For that is what he has done, Amelia. Unbeknownst to anyone except his mother, apparently, my Lord Westwick has married his cousin Sophie, the one who came to stay with Lady Westwick to comfort her after the death of the old lord. They have "fallen in love." Spare me from such maudlin sentiment! Fallen in love, indeed. My lord assured me that he had the greatest respect for me, etc., etc. He assured me that he had tried on the occasion of his last visit to explain the situation to me, but had found himself unable to produce the necessary details. One may well imagine! I well remember that he spoke warmly of his cousin on that occasion. Oh, yes, he had indeed mentioned her and enlightened me as to his vast appreciation of her usefulness to his mama. She was all kindness, all goodness, all sympathy and gentleness. His encomiums made me quite ill.

Not having had the courage to face me with the truth on that occasion, he had acquired a special license and they were married last week. A week ago! And he has only just gathered the courage to tell my father of his treachery. And hear this his reasoning, Amelia, if you will. He was not convinced that I loved him, but was certain that his cousin did. He did not love me (though holding me in the highest regard, of course), and knew that he did love his cousin. He had hoped, you see, that I would guess the state of his emo-

*tions and release him from his promise when he spoke so
glowingly of his cousin! As though I would do any such
thing when the announcement of our betrothal had already
been made.*

*No man of honor would do what Carstairs has done. I
still can scarcely credit that he has told us the truth. Oh, I
regret that Mama allowed a delay in the marriage, for had
I married him and gone to the Hall, there would have been
no need for his cousin to come and throw out her lures. And
I overheard Mama and Papa talking when they thought I
had gone to bed this evening. Papa thinks it was the old
lord who insisted on Carstairs marrying, and Mama thinks
the dowager Lady Westwick did not care for me and pur-
posely arranged for her weasely little cousin to come and
attract Carstairs' notice. Both my parents, however, have
made it clear that if queried, I must indicate that it was I
who broke off the engagement. Otherwise, I shall look a
complete fool, Papa says, though I don't see it myself.
Carstairs is the villain of this piece, and I would have
everyone know it!*

There was a hastily written postscript that begged Amelia
Nowlin to keep the story to herself since Miss Longstreet's
parents were adamant about the necessity to have no word
of the true situation leak out.

"Oh, dear." Nell set the letter aside as though she wished
nothing to do with its contents. "How awful. I find it almost
impossible to believe that Lord Westwick could have done
such a thing."

Sir Hugh nodded, his face drawn. "And yet, I cannot believe that your aunt lied, or even exaggerated, in her letter.
He seems to have chosen to marry the woman he loved despite the heavy social penalty it might have brought him.
He was fortunate that Miss Longstreet's parents insisted on
her taking the blame. But it was grossly unfair to her, of
course. I think you may be right that your aunt is here in
Bath to seek revenge."

Nell felt tears prick at her eyes. "Poor Aunt Longstreet. She must have suffered dreadfully."

"At least the blow was to her pride and not to her heart," Sir Hugh remarked, his voice gentle. "She does not seem to have been 'in love' with the earl. And I must tell you that it has always been obvious that he was very much in love with his wife, and she with him, to the day of her death."

"So I understand." Nell clasped her hands tightly in her lap, a frown wrinkling her brow. "Do you suppose it was a self-imposed exile, his living here in Bath rather than staying on his estate in Westmorland?"

"Probably. He must have thought it the least (and perhaps the most) he could do to make amends to my godmother and her parents—to stay as far away from them as possible."

"And so he built a new life here, and no one has ever known about that broken engagement." Nell glanced over at Sir Hugh. "But, of course, Mrs. Dorsey must have known all about it. She would have gotten a letter, much like your mother's, when it happened."

The baronet nodded. "I'm sure she did, since she told you your aunt had once been engaged to the earl. She will be part of your aunt's plot to be avenged for the destruction of her expectations. Should we try to speak to Mrs. Dorsey?"

Nell felt torn. Once again, it would be calling her loyalty into question if she did anything to stand in her aunt's way, and yet of course she must. No matter what Lord Westwick had done, it was many years ago, and he was an older man now. The social disgrace would be intolerable, and so unnecessary. "Yes, of course we must speak with Mrs. Dorsey. I doubt she has any idea what's afoot. For that matter, you and I can only suspect what Aunt Longstreet plans. And what about Lord Westwick? Should you speak with him?"

"Do you wish me to?"

Nell sighed. "Oh, Hugh, I don't know. He must still feel the shame of his actions, even if he has never regretted them. He won't like it that we know. Especially you. He is excessively fond of you."

Her companion scowled and flicked a finger against the remaining letters he held. "What an unpleasant interview *that* would be. And it might cause some damage to . . . to persons who wouldn't seem to be involved."

Nell regarded him questioningly.

Hugh looked uncomfortable. "He spoke of some plans he had, which I am not at liberty to disclose. It might be best if we said nothing for the time being."

"I can't think that's right," Nell argued. "Difficult as it might be, he should know what we've learned."

"Perhaps." The baronet tapped a finger restlessly on his chair arm. "Would you let me think about this, Nell? Let me consider the ramifications?"

"But . . ."

"Please. Just overnight."

Nell could not understand his hesitation, but he looked so earnest and so concerned that she capitulated. "Very well. Until tomorrow."

When he rose, she stood also, but indicated the remaining letters. "What of those? Did you not wish me to read them?"

A slight flush tinted his cheeks. "I'll leave them with you. Some of them concern your mother, others Miss Longstreet's . . . ah . . . role as my godmother."

Nell reached out a hand for the aging sheets of paper. Her fingers brushed his, and she felt an unaccustomed flutter in her chest. Briefly, so briefly that she might have imagined it, he clasped and pressed her fingers before letting them go. "Thank you," she said. "I shall take good care of them."

"Miss Armstrong . . . Nell . . . I was loath to withhold any of your aunt's letters, but you must remember that some of them were written at the height of your grandparents' anxiety about your mother. Your grandmother was always a conciliating and generous woman, but your grandfather . . . Well, let us say that he was not always reasonable, and that on occasion his judgments were harsh and unfair. I remember that as a lad; you probably encountered it as a young lady."

Keeping her eyes on the letters in her hands, she nodded. "He could be a harsh man on occasion."

A note of anger crept into Sir Hugh's voice when he said, "I would not forgive him if he was ever harsh with you."

"No, no, not harsh. He was . . . unforgiving of my mother, you see, and therefore could never accept me as I should have liked."

"Well," he said gruffly, "read the letters, but do not despair over them. They were penned a good many years ago, and time would have softened the worst of his attitudes, I daresay."

Nell smiled faintly. "Perhaps, but I shan't be surprised if I recognize them."

"Poor dear," Hugh murmured.

"Nonsense," she said stoutly. "I am a fortunate young woman to have been accepted into the family home. I might well have been placed in an orphanage and trained to domestic service when my parents died, sir. I hope you will spare no pity for me."

He regarded her stubbornly thrust-out chin and laughed. "Oh, no. Pity is the last thing I feel for you, my dear Nell."

And he was gone, before she could do more than blink at him.

Because her aunt might return at any moment, Nell carried the letters up to her bedchamber. It was a pretty room, with dainty furniture and wispy curtains. She moved immediately to the window, which looked out on the square, and was fortunate enough to see the baronet just disappearing around the corner onto Gay Street.

What had he meant by that: "Pity is the last thing I feel for you, my dear Nell"? She touched her fingers to her lips and allowed herself to drift into a daydream where the baronet was escorting her to a ball. She was dressed in her emerald gown, and he was resplendent in his most elegant evening clothes with a cravat so starched and shining that his face rose above it like a portrait. The strains of the music just reached her, and she felt a thrill when she realized it was a waltz they played. He took her in his arms and effortlessly guided her about the dance floor. And though there was a scent of jasmine and the glow of a thousand candles in gleaming chandeliers, they were the only people on the floor. His hand at her waist so intimate, so confident. Whirling about until she was dizzy with the movement and the nearness to him . . .

Nell's lovely daydream was dispelled by a loud hammering on the front door. She gazed down to see that her aunt had returned and was demanding entrance in her best fashion. Nell sighed, slipped the letters into a drawer under her reticule, and went down to greet her aunt.

Hugh thought best when he rode, so he went directly home from Queen Square to change into his riding clothes. He instructed that his horse be brought around, and found himself within half an hour south of Bath and galloping across parkland. Despite the beauty of the day, and the interest of his surroundings, his thoughts never seemed to veer from Nell.

He wished there had been some way he could protect Nell from the mean-spirited nature of many of the comments in the letters he had left with her. His godmother was in the habit of quoting her papa on the subject of Margaret's elopement and the legitimacy—or lack thereof—of Nell's own birth.

More, he was not sure it was in her best interests to let Lord Westwick know of her having read those old letters. Would he be so inclined to find a way to give her an independence if he thought she held him in contempt? Not that she would, of course. Nell had been shocked by the revelation, but she was far too openhearted a young lady to completely change her good opinion of the earl on the basis of that one—admittedly distressing—action of his.

But there was her loyalty to her aunt. Had she not instantly sympathized with Rosemarie Longstreet at the destruction of her hopes and plans? This, despite her knowledge of her aunt's irascible nature. Of course, Hugh admitted as he slowed his horse to a walk when they approached a stand of trees, that irascible nature had no doubt been aided by the earl's rejection of her when she was young.

Hugh had not been born at the time of that event. And even as a boy coming to Longstreet Manor, he had not suffered from it. As a young man she had seemed to take him in dislike, and Hugh could now see that her disappointment and the memory of her own betrayal were at work. He well remembered receiving a letter from her excoriating him on his behavior toward one particular young woman. "You have raised her hopes of an offer!" Miss Longstreet scolded. "Your carelessness and cruelty could ruin her life!" Of course, his godmother had not had an intimate association with this particular courtship, where in fact he had been rather casually dismissed by the young lady in question, rather than the other way around. But Miss Longstreet had not forgotten—or forgiven, apparently.

As he was emerging from the small wood, Hugh saw his brother-in-law approaching along the road below. Once again, he was south of town and not on the western side,

where someone coming from Bristol might have been expected. Hugh drew his horse to a stop and stayed in the
shadow of the trees in order to watch where John Holmsly
went.

Hugh was familiar with the horses the Holmslys had
brought to Bath, since he had ridden out with Emily and
Nell on so many occasions. John was not riding one of
them. In fact, Hugh could have sworn that the horse he was
riding was the one that Hugh himself had ridden when he
visited Combe Park with Nell. Had his financial situation
been more robust, he might have made the earl an offer for
the stallion, but he had learned to be cautious in his expenditures.

John Holmsly appeared to be putting the horse through
his paces. He was not merely out riding, but using the
stretch of road below as a proving ground. Back and forth
he went, urging the horse to walk, to trot, to canter, to gallop. Reining the animal in to test his obedience. Encouraging him to accept the pressure of a heel or the tightening of
a rein as instruction. Hugh frowned down on the scene, per-
plexed. Was John planning to buy the animal? It looked almost as though he were training him.

Why? If it was indeed Lord Westwick's horse, and be-
longed at Combe Park, why would John be working with
the horse on this stretch of road? Hugh had the greatest hes-
itancy about confronting his brother-in-law. The man had a
right to his privacy, and he no doubt had a perfectly legitimate reason for being where he was and doing what he was
doing, but Hugh couldn't imagine what it would be.

Did Emily know where John was? In all likelihood she
did not, as evidenced by her frequent complaints about her
husband's absence and lack of information on his dealings.
And Hugh was reminded that both Nell and Hopkins had
told him they'd seen John Holmsly in this area, on different

occasions. Which suggested that John made a habit of being in the area, didn't it?

And not in Bristol, as he claimed.

Hugh had just made up his mind to confront his brother-in-law when he realized that John had ridden off. Hugh was not certain which of the three directions below was the correct one to follow, and so he abandoned his intent and, more puzzled than ever, returned to Bath.

Chapter Fifteen

When Nell had settled her aunt into a chair in the front parlor, covered her legs with a warm rug, and seen her drift off to sleep, she returned to her room. She pulled the old sheets of paper from her drawer and once again set herself to read the faded ink. The dates on the letters were widely spaced, but none appeared to be missing. Aunt Longstreet only wrote when there was some important news to convey.

As though we didn't have enough to bear here, she scribbled in one quick note, *now my sister Margaret has run off with a local farmer!*

Nell knew that this was an exaggeration. It was true that her father had been the son of a small farmer, and not a prosperous landowner, but he had been educated and was intended for the clergy. No one could have been less suited to such work, and he had made an effort to find some other occupation that would more closely match his talents. Unfortunately, his was a lighthearted nature, one given to the joyous living of each day as it came. His true talent lay in coaxing others to share in his enjoyment, a talent that was not easily aligned with remunerative employment. He had been fairly proficient, Nell remembered, in selling goods, including her mother's jewelry when things got particularly desperate.

There was Aunt Longstreet's letter that announced:

*My father has disowned Margaret. He cannot find that
she married Mr. Armstrong, and he believes they are living
in sin. Mama is distraught, and my spirits are decidedly low.
He was such an amusing boy, Mr. Armstrong. At the assemblies he would tease all the girls and flirt with the married
women. He could make anyone laugh, and I remember a
time when he even had old lady Wilson chortling. Not that
he should have aspired to someone of Margaret's birth, but
he was an amusing rascal.*

There were eventually letters about Sir Hugh's birth and
the choice of Aunt Longstreet as godmother to him. Letters
making arrangements for him to visit Longstreet Manor for
the summer, plans for making him heir to the property. Years
later there was a note that announced her own birth:

*Margaret has written me—she will not write my father—
that she has given birth to a daughter named Helen. Papa
refuses to acknowledge the birth and insists it would have
been better had the child never been born. Mama is anxious
to see her only grandchild, but Papa will not allow it.*

And there was eventually the brief note expressing Aunt
Longstreet's profound sense of loss when her mother died.
Shortly after that the letters stopped. Nell realized that Sir
Hugh's mother must have died then, and these letters were
bundled away.

She sat for a long time with the correspondence spread
around her on the bed. Since the letters had stopped before
her own parents died and she came to Longstreet Manor, she
had no idea of her aunt's feelings about that eventuality. Her
grandmother was already gone, so Nell suspected that it was
Aunt Longstreet's influence which had brought her to the
manor. Had the decision been left to her grandfather, she
might well have ended in an orphanage. But he had already
been failing, and whether her aunt had brought her there to

take care of the old man, or because she genuinely wished to welcome her niece, Nell could not then or now be certain. She only knew that she was grateful to have been taken in.

Gathering the sheets of aging paper together, Nell experienced a little guilt at having caught this glimpse into her aunt's life. She knew very well that her aunt would not like it one bit that not only Nell but Sir Hugh had read all of her letters to his mother. But Nell reminded herself that she would not have done it save for her concern about Aunt Longstreet's suspicious activities regarding Lord Westwick.

And what was Nell to do about that? She could—and would—warn the earl of what her aunt might have in mind, but there was really no way to stop the older woman if she was determined. Nothing would be simpler in the Bath society, Nell had observed, than to ruin someone's reputation with a few well-chosen words—especially if they were backed up by a trustworthy woman such as Mrs. Dorsey.

And why had Sir Hugh insisted that Nell give him a day to consider the consequences of speaking with Lord Westwick? What else was there to do? Oh, it had all become so complicated that Nell was developing the headache—and she could hear her aunt's strident voice calling for her from the parlor. With a sigh she returned the letters to her drawer and hastened down the stairs.

When Hugh stopped by his sister's house that evening and inquired for her husband, he was told that Mr. Holmsly was gone to Bristol. "And Mrs. Holmsly?" he asked the butler.

"Madame is with the child, Sir Hugh. He has a cough, and she decided to stay home to care for him."

Sir Hugh said he would make his own way to the nursery, and when he did so, he found his sister rocking and singing a lullaby to her son. When she caught sight of him, she placed a finger to her lips, singing, "Dear sir, not a peep, not a peep. This little baby is almost asleep. Where he'll dream of clouds and trees and dogs and bees and awake in the morning to . . . creep!"

Suppressing a laugh, the baronet moved back into the shadows of the large, sparsely furnished nursery and watched his sister with her son. It was a remarkable sight. Emily, so vivacious and eager among her contemporaries, was quiet and tender with the child. She stroked his hair and kissed his brow as she laid him in his crib, and stood for several minutes gazing down at him. Then slowly she backed up, watching to see if he would waken. Finally, she gestured to her brother that they should leave the room.

Only when the door was closed behind them did she speak. "Walter hasn't been feeling well. I know it is only a cough, but he seems calmer when I'm around. Besides, I hadn't much interest in going to Mrs. Grimshaw's card party, though I hope I haven't left her numbers uneven. And what brings you here, Hugh?"

As she spoke she turned and led him toward the little room she'd set aside for writing letters. There was a small *bergère* that she chose and a comfortable tub chair beside it for him. "I had thought John and I might be cozy in here," she remarked with a wistful sigh. "I would be surprised if he's been in this room above twice since we've been in Bath."

"He does seem to have been remarkably busy," Hugh said, cautious. "And not very communicative about his business, I gather."

"Ha! One would think he were involved in something illegal." Emily's eyes pooled with unshed tears. "You don't think he is, do you, Hugh?"

"Of course not. You mustn't let your imagination run wild, my dear."

"I try not to. But he is so secretive, it is hard not to wonder why. Could he not confide in his wife? The only reason

I can think of that he would not is because . . . because he is ashamed of what he's doing."

"Nonsense. Emily, most men think their wives shouldn't be burdened with the details of their business dealings. You know that."

"But John seems different now than he did when we married. Have you noticed it, Hugh?"

Hugh didn't know how to answer her. He certainly wasn't ready to tell her about seeing John that afternoon. "I think your husband is the same man he has always been, but perhaps he has concerns which are distracting him. I shall make an effort to get him to confide in me, Emily, though that won't mean I'll be able to tell tales to you. I can, however, do my best to assist him with whatever troubles him."

"I would be so grateful, Hugh. He'll listen to you."

Hugh somehow doubted that, but he was ready to deal with the other matter he'd come to discuss. "Mrs. Luther found my godmother's letters to Mama and sent them along."

Emily's brows rose in query. "And what did you discover?"

Hugh sighed. "More than I could have wished." And he proceeded to tell her, in broad outline, just what had happened between Lord Westwick and Miss Longstreet all those years ago. Emily looked disbelieving, and then distressed, and finally confused.

"You think your godmother has some intention of disgracing the earl?" she asked, incredulous.

"I very much fear she does. It was Nell's original concern about what Miss Longstreet was up to that had me send for the letters, and certainly one can see why she would be up to mischief in light of their revelations."

"But why would she have waited so long?"

Hugh shrugged. "Her father had made her act as though she broke the engagement. And then, of course, the earl's wife died only last year. One hesitates to suggest that Miss Longstreet was prohibited by the countess's presence, but it must certainly seem easier to carry out her plan now that Lady Westwick is gone."

"True. Even the Bath quizzes would have hesitated to excoriate Lord Westwick when his wife was alive."

"And do you think they will now?" Hugh asked.

"They're fickle; they might." Emily's chin came up. "But I shan't. The earl has been kind to me, and I certainly will not cut him, or make any change at all in how I approach him."

Her brother smiled. "Good girl! I'm sure it will help to have a few people stand by him."

"Have you told him about the letters?"

"No, but I plan to before the assembly tomorrow. Since my godmother has invited Mrs. Dorsey to join us, I'm certain that's when she plans to set her scandal in motion."

"You know, Hugh, it was very wrong of him. No wonder Miss Longstreet is such an ogre. I would have been devastated if John had done something like that to me."

"I fancy Westwick tried to get out of the engagement by hinting to Miss Longstreet that he'd fallen in love with his cousin, but she either did not understand or refused to accept the situation. And I think his father was exerting pressure on him to ally the two families, while his mother was very much against it and threw his cousin in his way after his father's death. Of course it was wrong, but I see him as a torn and confused young man, trying to please everyone and obviously being unable to do so."

"Yes, and though he ended up doing what he felt compelled to do, he must have suffered severely for the loss of his honor. Leaving his estate in that fashion would have been excessively difficult. Think how you would feel about leaving Fallings forever."

"I *have* thought of it, my dear." An understatement, Hugh

knew, but he was not willing to burden his sister with his financial problems. It occurred to him then, and for the first time, that John Holmsly might be doing precisely the same thing. Hugh was not aware of Holmsly having financial problems, but what more likely explanation for his odd behavior?

What did a young man of Holmsly's position do if he needed to refill the family coffers, provided he was not a gambler or a thief? Hugh *knew* Holmsly wasn't a gambler, and he assumed his brother-in-law was not a thief. Emily was regarding him curiously, and he said, "I need to do some hard thinking about all this, Emily. I know you'll do your best to see that Nell doesn't suffer from her aunt's vindictiveness. I should hate to see her tarred with the same brush her aunt will be. For people will believe Miss Longstreet, I have no doubt, but they will also scorn her for having brought this old disgrace up and forcing them to take sides against a man they've always respected."

"I shall consider it just one more reason that Nell should come to live with me!"

Hugh gave her a long, penetrating look and said, "I don't think that will be necessary."

Emily stared at him, but said only, "Oh."

"Good night, Emily. I hope Walter is perfectly well by morning."

"Thank you. I feel certain he shall be."

Chapter Sixteen

Nell had expected to visit Mrs. Dorsey as soon as Sir Hugh called the next day. But Sir Hugh did not call. Instead, about midday there was a note from him advising her that Lord Westwick was not at home and would not return at least until evening. *So, please,* he wrote, *take no action. We can hope that he won't attend the Lower Rooms and therefore won't be the object of your aunt's vengeance.*

Whether Lord Westwick came to the rooms or not was immaterial, so far as Nell was concerned. Rosemarie Longstreet did not need the man's presence to start spreading her tale of his duplicity and broken promises. All she needed was Mrs. Dorsey's verification of her story, and Mrs. Dorsey would most certainly be there. Nell chafed under the need to take some action, but her aunt was proving particularly demanding that afternoon and made it difficult for Nell to slip away from Queen Square.

What Rosemarie wanted was for Nell to work on her aunt's gown to make it look more fashionable. "You've looked at the fashion plates," her aunt insisted. "You know what is in style today. Surely you can do something with my gown, if you have some help from my dresser."

"But, Aunt Longstreet, the fabric is the major difficulty. It's so heavy and stiff that it doesn't lend itself to the wispy, flowing designs they're wearing now. Perhaps if you were to wear an open robe of a lighter material over it, with your gown as a petticoat . . ."

"I cannot think that would be at all flattering," Rosemarie protested. "I wish to appear to advantage this evening."

"Is there any particular reason for that?" Nell asked, not meeting her aunt's gaze, but continuing to contemplate the dress hanging before her.

"Why shouldn't I wish to appear to advantage? You will be wearing the green gown again, I suppose. You might as well get as much service from it as you can before we return to Westmorland."

"Perhaps Mrs. Dorsey has a gown she would be willing to lend you. The two of you are of a size. I could run 'round to her house and find out."

"Nonsense. I will not be reduced to wearing someone else's clothing."

"Hmm." Nell stepped back from the gown and turned to consider her aunt. "There is a shop on Milsom Street where I have seen some particularly handsome India scarves. Worn across the shoulder like so . . ." Nell proceeded to demonstrate with an old shawl she plucked from her aunt's wardrobe. "You might look quite fashionable. However, the scarves were very dear."

Rosemarie narrowed her eyes. "How dear?"

"There was one for three guineas . . ."

"Three guineas! You're mad."

Nell shrugged. "Some were more expensive, some less. I could take you there to see if any of them appealed to you."

Her aunt snorted. "As though I would be willing to spend three guineas on an India scarf! But perhaps I could look at them. These shopkeepers are notorious for overcharging. I could talk them into lowering their prices."

Though Nell very much doubted that, she sighed and agreed to accompany her aunt.

Under gloomy skies the two women walked briskly to

Milsom Street, as her aunt saw no reason for dawdling, and her gout, whether because of the waters or simply on its own, had abated. She once again professed her astonishment when Nell pointed out the scarves in the shopwindow and told her what prices they were.

Her aunt regarded her suspiciously. "Why did you go in to find out their cost? Surely you had no intention of purchasing such an expensive item."

Nell flushed. "I had rather hoped they were more reasonably priced."

"You've been beguiled by the glamour in this town," her aunt scolded. "It's a good thing we won't be staying here much longer."

This was news to Nell. "When had you intended to leave, Aunt Longstreet?"

"Soon, very soon. My gout is gone, isn't it? What other reason could prolong my stay in Bath?"

What indeed? "I'm a little concerned . . ." Nell began.

But her aunt was already pushing open the shop door. A bell tinkled excitedly, and within the dark interior Nell could see the shopkeeper already moving forward, a smile firmly planted on his face. "In what way may I be of assistance, ladies?" he asked, all unsuspecting.

"I'm interested in an India scarf," Rosemarie declared, "like those in the window. Nothing expensive." Nell hovered behind her aunt, near the door, where she might make a hasty retreat.

The man seemed taken aback. "They are very fine scarves, madam, shipped directly from India and made of the finest materials. I believe they are priced quite reasonably."

"You do, do you?" Her aunt directed an imperious finger toward the most opulent of the lot. "How much, for instance, would that one cost?"

"Four guineas. But, madam, that is the finest of them all.

This one," he said, running a hand lovingly along the soft fabric, "is three guineas."

"Four guineas! Three guineas! You should be ashamed of yourself. Why, I daresay the poor heathen who wove them didn't earn a ha'penny."

"I'm sure I wouldn't know about such things," the man said stiffly. "But I assure madam that they are worth every penny of their price. You wouldn't find finer quality material or workmanship even in London. The most select items find their way to my shop. Ladies from all over the kingdom come to me for their India scarves. If you are not interested in the first quality, I can recommend a shop farther down the hill which will satisfy you."

Rosemarie did not like having the tables turned on her. She would not admit to being in search of lesser quality than the best, but she was determined not to pay such exorbitant fees. She glared at the man before picking up each of the scarves in turn and examining it minutely. "How much is this one?" she asked finally, holding up a beautiful gray scarf with red, yellow, and blue threads in a soft, fanciful design.

"Two guineas."

"Oh, really?" Her eyes narrowed, and she turned the scarf over to exhibit a snag that had pulled the material into a bunch in one spot. "For defective merchandise? And you claim to be a purveyor of quality goods!"

The man reached out to take the scarf from her. After examining the material, he set the scarf aside. "It is a small flaw, indeed, but I do not sell damaged merchandise. I will remove it from the display."

"I would be willing to purchase it for a guinea," Rosemarie informed him.

"A guinea!" The man shook his head. "No, no, madam. Even damaged, it is worth a great deal more than that."

The two bickered for several minutes before settling on a price that Rosemarie was willing, if not pleased, to pay.

"Here, Helen," she said, waving the package triumphantly, "you shall carry it for me. Carefully, now. We don't want any *more* damage to it."

Nell could only be grateful when the shop door had closed behind them. Acknowledging her aunt's persistence and determination, she decided there was really no sense in attempting to dissuade her from whatever course she had chosen for the evening. Best to let it happen and get it over with, no matter how distressing it proved to be.

The flambeaux outside the Assembly Rooms cast bright light on the gleaming carriages, and allowed deep shadows beyond them. If it hadn't been for her worry about her aunt's plans, Nell would have felt like a princess that evening. She was aware of being fashionably dressed, of being escorted by a man as elegant as any she had known—and of an emotion in her heart for him that nearly overwhelmed her.

The hard reality was that she had fallen in love with Sir Hugh, as impractical and presumptuous as that was. Back at home in Westmorland, she might fantasize about being with him—as she had done so many times with imaginary men—but this man was real, and all her daydreaming would not bring him back into her life. As he gripped her hand to assist her from his carriage, Nell allowed herself to smile at him in an unguarded way to express the gratitude she felt toward him for his thoughtfulness and his care of her. In return she felt the pressure on her fingers and thought that he perhaps intended to lift them to his lips.

But there was Aunt Longstreet leaning forward, muttering, "What is taking so long? Have you no consideration for an old lady's sensibilities? We are still cooped up in this cramped space, you know."

Sir Hugh sighed and smiled his regret before stepping up to the carriage to offer his assistance. Her aunt grumbled and made sarcastic remarks, but once she and Mrs. Dorsey were safely on the pavement, she linked arms with her friend, raised her head high, and strode stiff-backed into the building. Nell and Sir Hugh were left to follow behind.

"Lord Westwick did not return all day," he told her in an undertone. "Did you speak with Mrs. Dorsey?"

"No. Even if I had thought it necessary, I was given no opportunity. Aunt Longstreet kept me close by her all day."

"And you're still convinced something will happen this evening?"

"Absolutely." Nell watched as her aunt's pelisse was removed and her friend's redingote taken. "Today she mentioned that we would be leaving Bath very soon now."

Sir Hugh's brows drew down. "I very much wish that you could be spared this evening's brouhaha, Nell."

"Nonsense," Nell retorted bracingly. "At least I am a little prepared, and have a good understanding of my aunt's situation. Poor Mrs. Dorsey is the one you should feel sorry for."

"I do," he admitted with a rueful grin.

Rosemarie Longstreet's India scarf looked very well with her gown, Nell thought, and did indeed seem to soften the old-fashioned cut and fabric somewhat. Nell had plucked off half the ornamentation on her aunt's headdress, so the oval shape and the satin torsade on the rolled brim were evident. Though her aunt had complained bitterly, she was mollified when Mrs. Dorsey complimented her on her hat.

Her aunt stood in the doorway to the ballroom for some moments, observing the crowd with a careful eye. At length she gave a brisk nod and said to her friend, "Come, Mrs. Dorsey. I believe I recognize someone across the room. And, Helen," she said, turning back, "you run along and enjoy yourself with your friends. I won't be needing your assistance."

Nell knew better than to argue with her, but she raised troubled eyes to Hugh as her aunt moved away. "We need someone to watch what she's about."

"Right you are." He in turn gazed about the room. "We shall enlist Emily's sister-in-law in the cause. You met Mrs. Billings at the concert."

Mrs. Billings scarcely blinked an eye at being asked to spy on Hugh's godmother. One would have thought, Nell decided, that it was not at all out of the ordinary for her to be approached on just such a mission. And though Nell was distracted by Hugh's insistence that she stand up with him "to assure your aunt that you're out of the way," she could not help casting anxious glances in the direction of the older women.

It was difficult for Nell to divide her attention between the newly learned steps of the dance and her aunt across the room. Oh, how she would have loved to give herself over to the pleasure of dancing with Hugh! When she looked in his eyes, as Emily had taught her to do when she danced, there seemed to be a special light, a definite gleam of appreciation or—or something. His regard was so intense, so captivating, that she might almost have believed he cared for her.

Then suddenly she saw Mrs. Billings, her face pinched with worry, motioning them from the dance. Nell's gaze flew to her companion. Sir Hugh, already aware of Mrs. Billings' summons, excused them by murmuring that the overheated rooms were making his partner a little faint. Nell had no difficulty feigning distress to back up his statement, and soon Mrs. Billings was waving her fan before Nell's face. But in an urgent undertone, she said, "Oh, you will not believe what she is saying! I could scarce believe my ears!"

"I'm very much afraid we know precisely what she's saying," Hugh replied grimly, as he, too, continued the pretense of ministering to Nell by rubbing her hands vigorously.

Mrs. Billings looked startled, but continued. "She is telling Lady Vanen that Lord Westwick married another woman while affianced to her! And Mrs. Dorsey, poor little bird, when called upon to verify the account, is unable to disagree."

Nell grimaced at this confirmation of her worst fears. Pulling her hands away from Hugh, she said, "I shall go to her and see whether I can stem the tide."

"I'm afraid it's too late for that," Mrs. Billings sighed. And then, with a stricken look, she gestured toward the doorway. "Oh, lord. And here is the earl now."

The Earl of Westwick had paused at the edge of the room to get his bearings. His appearance only made the word spread faster around the room. Nell could see that a dozen eyes were trained on him, even as lady whispered to gentleman, and partner whispered to partner. An odd hush occurred for just a moment, before the buzz of conversation rose louder than ever. The musicians in the orchestra apse above the entrance struck up the next number, but there was a strange lack of couples to make up the line of the dance.

"I would have left him a note," Hugh said sadly, "but it seemed impossible to explain the situation other than face-to-face. And I did not think he would return to town in time to attend this evening."

Nell found herself on her feet. "Bring him to Aunt Longstreet, Hugh." Then, remembering that his inheritance depended on his remaining on terms with her aunt, she amended, "Or I can."

"I'll bring him."

As Hugh moved off toward the earl, Nell hastened toward her aunt, who was seated on one of the settees, surrounded by a bevy of ogling ladies and gentlemen. Oh, she looked so satisfied, and poor Mrs. Dorsey so miserable, that Nell could scarcely keep the angry tears from pricking at her eyes. Turning to Mrs. Billings, who had followed her, she said, "Would you take Mrs. Dorsey for a cup of tea, ma'am?"

"With pleasure."

In a moment Nell was left standing alone in front of her

aunt, though there was a whole press of folk almost within hearing distance. In a lowered voice she said, "So this is what you've been planning, Aunt Longstreet. I hope it has given you some satisfaction, for it will certainly be the cause of great distress to several people. And I trust it atones for the slight you received years ago."

Nell sighed and shook her head unhappily. "How sad that you suffered so much and could not put it behind you. Your life might have been far otherwise without the bitterness and the rancor."

"It was not I who behaved dishonorably," Rosemarie snapped. *"There* is the villain of the piece. *There* is the man who dashed my hopes and ruined my life."

Lord Westwick had indeed arrived at Nell's side, his face set. He made a stiff, formal bow to Miss Longstreet and gave Nell a small, apologetic smile. "Yes," he agreed in a lowered voice, "I am the villain of the piece. No one is to blame except myself. And I must thank you, Rosemarie, for waiting until my dear wife died before carrying out this punishment. It was generous to a fault of you, and more than I would have dared plead for."

Rosemarie colored up in a most unbecoming way. "I didn't do it for you, you imbecile!"

"No, of course you didn't. Nonetheless, my wife was spared the disgrace you have so obviously planned for me, and I cannot but feel a vast relief."

"I don't want your thanks! Don't speak to me!" Rosemarie turned her head aside, as if she could block him thus from her vision.

"Still," he said with a gentle smile, "you have it. And more, you have my willingness to fulfill my promise now, at this late date, if you should have any desire for my hand."

Nell regarded the pair in stunned silence. Then her aunt thumped her cane viciously against the floor and cried, "You are merely trying to reclaim your honor! You want these people to think what you did was not so wrong, since you are willing to come around now. Nonsense! That's ludicrous! Who wants to marry an old man? You were young once, and vigorous. Now look at you! And look at me. I would be a laughing stock to marry at my age."

Nell hastened to murmur, "No one is ever a laughing stock to marry where she chooses, Aunt."

"I don't choose to marry him! I hate him! I have detested him from the moment he broke his word to me." She turned on the earl and growled, "We would have had children. I know we would. You would not be heirless if you had married me."

"Possibly not. It was perhaps a price, one of many, that I paid for breaking my word." Lord Westwick crouched down beside her, attempting to place a hand over hers. Rosemarie pulled her hand away as though he had burned her.

The earl persisted. "Rosemarie, I would have married you if you had loved me. Even though I'd fallen in love with my cousin, I would have married you, kept my word, if I had known you to cherish me as I cherished my Sophie. Because those two things—my word and your love—would have outweighed our own, Sophie's and mine. But you didn't love me, Rosemarie, and I wasn't willing to break Sophie's heart to fulfill my word. It is as simple as that—and as wretched. I am very, very sorry to have ruined your life, but I didn't expect that, you see. I believed you would go on to find a love of your own and marry him and be happy."

"Where was I to find someone to love?" she demanded, irate. "In the middle of nowhere! And what is love after all but a chimera—here today, gone tomorrow, a bit of folktale and magic. It doesn't last. There is nothing to it but a syrupy sentiment which I would never subscribe to, believe me."

"It's true that not everyone finds love," Westwick admitted. "And it's true that what is called love does not always last. But the depth of my feelings for my wife lasted through our entire marriage. And though I cannot speak for Sophie, I believe she felt the same."

He shook his head sadly, attempting again to touch her hand. This time Aunt Longstreet pushed his hand away with her cane in a petulant, slightly less vigorous manner. The earl sighed. "Oh, Rosemarie, I would that things had been different, that there had been some way to divide myself in two, to honor my word and my heart. But you were young and pretty and seemed to me well able to command the hand of any man you wished."

"I had accepted your hand."

"Yes, you had. I can't do anything to make up for that now, I'm afraid, except offer you my hand again. It's an old hand, as you say, but not infirm as yet. Nor do you look ready for the grave, my dear. We might spend a few good years together."

"Ha!" she snorted. "Here in Bath where all these old tabbies would forever compare me to your wife? At your estate in Westmorland where your heir would have to be displaced? I don't think so."

"I had in mind that we would live at Longstreet Manor."

"You had no such thing in mind," she snapped, her eyes glaring fiercely at him. "When you came here tonight, you had no more intention of offering me your hand in marriage—*again!*—than you did of flying."

His eyes danced. "You'll never know that for sure, will you, Rosemarie? Especially since you will find on your return to Queen Square that there is a package of documents there for you delivered by my man of business. These are matters I only concluded today, though they have been in the works for some time. One of them is contingent on your marrying me, but the others—" He shrugged. "Shall we say that I have managed to circumvent you should you prove stubborn."

"This is all nonsense," she muttered, though she looked

uncertain. "What possible dealings could you have with me?"

"An assembly is not the proper place to discuss this," he insisted. "Shall we adjourn to Queen Square, or to the Parade? Or perhaps a neutral location, such as your godson's apartments in the Crescent?"

"You just want to get me away from here so I can't tell any more people about your infamous behavior."

"I'm sure you've told enough people that the word will spread far and wide, Rosemarie. But if you would prefer to spend the evening ensuring its dispersal, we can discuss our business tomorrow."

"I have no intention of ever discussing anything with you," she snapped.

Nell felt it incumbent upon her to intervene at this juncture. "Aunt Longstreet, I must tell you that I have no intention of staying here to witness your destruction of Lord Westwick's reputation. I'm sure you feel justified in your revenge, but I cannot be a party to it. And I'm sure Mrs. Dorsey is mortified to be your unwitting assistant. If Sir Hugh would be so good, I would beg him to convey me home."

"Where is your family loyalty?" demanded Rosemarie. "How can you fail to support me when I have provided a roof over your head and the very food you eat? Ungrateful child."

"Come, Aunt Longstreet. You know I'm grateful for your kindness, but you cannot expect me to condone behavior which I find uncalled for and unnecessary. Lord Westwick has expressed his regret at having caused so much distress in your life. He made a difficult decision. Would you have had him marry you when he was in love with another woman?"

Though the answer was undoubtedly yes, Nell knew that her aunt would find such a confession humiliating. "Oh, love," her aunt snorted. "Love is blamed for all manner of follies. Look at your own mother, running off with a farmer's son because she was 'in love.' Bah."

"Perhaps you would not be so scornful if you had ev⟨er⟩ been in love," Nell suggested.

"And what could you possibly know of love?" her aur⟨t⟩ asked. "It's no more real than one of your daydreams, missy Just a girlish fancy."

Nell blushed but refused to be intimidated. "I suspect yo⟨u⟩ know that it is indeed real, Aunt, and that your true regret i⟨s⟩ that you've never felt it."

"Balderdash! Love has no place in the life of a lady ⟨of⟩ quality. At best it's an unruly emotion that aids not one wh⟨it⟩ in forwarding a family's future. You need look no furthe⟨r⟩ than your own mother. Affection is a great deal more impor⟨-⟩ tant in establishing a solid foundation for marriage. And I as⟨-⟩ sure you," she said, glaring once again at the earl, "that I fel⟨t⟩ a certain affection for my fiancé at the time I accepted hi⟨s⟩ offer of marriage."

"I'm gratified to hear it," he said with a low bow. "Rose⟨-⟩ marie, allow me to escort you home. We have a great deal t⟨o⟩ discuss in private."

Chapter Seventeen

Nell thought for a moment that her aunt was going to refuse. Her face was still set stubbornly, and her hands clenched tightly in her lap. But Mrs. Dorsey appeared beside her, dropping a hand on her shoulder and saying, "You know you need to hear what Lord Westwick has to say, Rosemarie. This is your opportunity to straighten out something that has ruined too much of your life. My son is forever counseling me to let bygones be bygones, not because it will help the other person, but because it will bring comfort to me."

Since Mrs. Dorsey's son was a minister, not one of her aunt's favorite occupations, this advice could not be supposed to have much influence with her. Yet Nell witnessed a softening of her aunt's expression. Perhaps it had occurred to her that the earl might actually have something worthwhile to say. Or perhaps she was merely tired of the whole scenario she had created. In any case, she said, "Very well. Sir Hugh may escort us home, and Lord Westwick may follow us."

Rosemarie had nothing to say on the ride back to Queen Square. Mrs. Dorsey was dropped at her home with a short exchange of pleasantries, but neither Sir Hugh nor Nell attempted to converse with their companion, who sat rod stiff against the comfortable squabs of Sir Hugh's carriage, staring straight ahead. However, when Hugh attempted to take his leave of the ladies at their house, Rosemarie barked, "You

are coming in with us. I may need you to throw Lord Wes
wick out."

Not very encouraging, Nell feared. And yet there was
packet of papers on the hall stand, as the earl had indicate
there would be. Her aunt frowned at them, picked them u|
and carried them to the parlor, saying to Woodbridge, "Brin|
more candles. No sense ruining our eyes."

Before they had even seated themselves, there was
knock at the door and Lord Westwick was shown into th
room. "Ah, good. If you would allow me to explain each o
them . . ."

Nell was stunned by what ensued. The earl had made pro
vision for her. Whether her aunt married him or not, he ha|
arranged that Nell should have ten thousand pounds. The in
come from such a sum would provide her with a handsom
allowance—enough to buy any gown she should care t(
have. Rosemarie was instantly suspicious. "And just why
would you find it necessary to provide a dowry for m|
niece?"

"Because you have not done so yourself, and because you|
father did not do so when he might have." Lord Westwicl
pursed his lips. "I feel indirectly responsible for your sister'
elopement, Rosemarie, though I daresay it had little enoug|
to do with my misbehavior toward you. Still, Margaret mus|
have been affected by the whole mess, or she would not hav(
done anything so rash."

"She was always an impulsive girl," Rosemarie declared.

Lord Westwick ignored the comment, but turned to Nell t(
say, "I have investigated the circumstances of your parents'
marriage, and found that it was performed in a small hamle
shortly after their elopement. Your father's family was apparently always aware of precisely what had taken place
unfortunately, your grandfather was not willing to communi-
cate with them in order to learn the truth of the matter. This
too, I hold myself partially to blame for, Miss Armstrong.

My actions seem to have given him a distrust of his daughters' beaux, which he found difficult to overcome, else he would no doubt have discovered the truth of the matter himself."

"But you're not responsible for me!" Nell protested. "I'm grateful that you've established my legitimacy, but there is no reason for you to take any financial burden upon yourself, my lord."

"Someone needs to," he said. "Your grandfather would have been the most appropriate person, but he does not seem to have made any push to provide you with an inheritance. I am without children of my own, Miss Armstrong. It pleases me to be in a position to provide for your future."

"I'm perfectly capable of providing for my niece," Rosemarie grumbled.

"And have you done so?" the earl asked.

"Not as yet."

"Which has made your niece dependent upon you, Rosemarie. And seeing this young woman dependent on the goodwill of a cantankerous lady is not a particularly appealing prospect to me, so I have taken matters into my own hands. Frankly, I consider your father's behavior toward Miss Armstrong reprehensible, and yours only slightly less so. Your insistence on family loyalty does not seem to have extended to your own niece. Miss Armstrong has done nothing but serve her family, to be rewarded with no more than a pittance of an allowance and the undistinguished role of poor relation."

"The property is promised to my godson," Rosemarie said in defense of herself. "That has been understood for many years."

Sir Hugh made no comment, but Lord Westwick gave a tsk of annoyance. "Surely you could have carved out a respectable portion for your niece, Rosemarie. The reason you did not do so, it seems to me, is because you preferred her bound to you. With an independence, she might have chosen to do something different with her life."

An unbecoming flush stained Rosemarie's face. "My niece stays with me because she is family, and because Longstreet Manor is her home."

Nell felt called upon to make some comment, yet she was not quite certain how she felt at the moment. Longstreet Manor *was* her home, but it had not always been a comfortable home. And she had not always felt welcome there, or indeed a true member of the family. Still, she said, "Aunt Longstreet has provided me with a home, Lord Westwick. She has never remarked on my legitimacy or lack thereof, and I have always been aware that her godson was destined to inherit the estate."

"And I," admitted Sir Hugh, "have become unconscionably alarmed by the certainty that Miss Armstrong is the logical person to inherit Longstreet Manor. My own expectations are nothing compared to her legitimate claims on the family estate."

Rosemarie regarded Sir Hugh with disfavor. "My father intended that you should have Longstreet Manor because you were my godson and he wished the property to go to a male. He did not believe in women owning estates, and considered the property merely in trust to you. I was only carrying out his wishes."

Lord Westwick sighed. "Your father, Rosemarie, was an opinionated, prejudiced, and irritating gentleman. I can see no reason why you should feel compelled to follow his wishes, but that is of no consequence. Miss Armstrong will be provided for, and Sir Hugh may claim his inheritance with a clear conscience. The only question left to be answered is whether you wish to marry me and live with me at Longstreet Manor."

"Why should I?"

The earl shrugged. "Because, my dear, we are two older

people who might make our peace and live comfortably together until we die."

"I have no intention of dying anytime soon."

"Nor do I."

Nell regarded her aunt with a deep question in her eyes. Could this woman, who had lived such a bitter life, do more than punish the earl were she to marry him? And was that why he offered her his hand now, to give her precisely that chance? She wanted to advise both of them against the wisdom of their marrying, but she knew her intervention would not be appropriate. She cast a helpless look at Sir Hugh.

He misunderstood her plea and addressed his godmother. "I trust that Miss Armstrong would have a home at Longstreet Manor, no matter what your decision, ma'am."

Rosemarie regarded him haughtily. "I cannot see that it is any business of yours, Sir Hugh. Of course Helen may live at Longstreet Manor for as long as she pleases, though with such a dowry as Westwick is offering her, she will doubtless be besieged by every fortune hunter in the kingdom."

Her gaze on him sharpened, almost in a challenging way, but he only said stiffly, "I'm pleased to hear Miss Armstrong will always have a home with you if that is her wish."

And then Rosemarie rose abruptly. "Enough. It's been a tiring evening, and I'm for my bed. I shall have to give a few days' consideration to my answer, Lord Westwick. Now take yourselves off, both of you."

Nell smiled sympathetically at each of the gentlemen in turn, then watched as they complied with her aunt's decree. Left alone with her, Nell thought they might discuss the issues that had arisen during the evening, but her aunt waved aside any attempt at conversation. "Tomorrow," she said. "Perhaps."

Nell followed her aunt up the stairs but her mind was so preoccupied that she almost forgot to turn into her own room. If Lord Westwick did not change his mind—and she could not imagine that he would—she was now independently wealthy. She could do what she wished, go where she chose, buy what caught her eye. Nell was not foolish enough to reject such a gift, and yet she could see that its very existence was something of a slap at her aunt and grandfather.

And what of her promise to her grandfather on his deathbed? If Aunt Longstreet chose to marry Lord Westwick, Nell might consider herself free of that vow, but if she did not . . .

Since Nell had told the maid not to wait up for her, she cautiously released herself from the beautiful emerald gown. She could have a dozen such dresses now, if she wished. But the emerald gown would always be special, because she had worn it with Sir Hugh.

She caught her reflection in the cheval glass. By candlelight her naked body seemed soft and ripe. She could almost imagine herself about to welcome her husband to her bed. Her breasts felt heavy with longing, her womb stirred with excitement. He would come to her, kiss her, touch her. She would feel his naked body twined with hers. And she would cry out in sheer joy at their union.

Nell turned away from her image and quickly drew a nightdress from the stand. Sir Hugh was merely her friend. Had he not made certain that she could remain with Aunt Longstreet at the Manor, no matter what her aunt's decision? Obviously he had no intention of providing a home for her himself.

Nell forced herself to accept this truth. Her daydreams of being with Sir Hugh were just that. He had indeed become her friend, as Emily had, over the past weeks in Bath. His concern about who was to inherit Longstreet Manor had been answered tonight. It would be his when Aunt Longstreet died. Though that was likely to be years from now, it was Nell's impression that that would be enough to revive the Nowlin fortunes. He had no need to marry an heiress as well.

She sighed as she extinguished her candle and climbed into the four-poster bed. Her life had changed today in a most surprising way. Heaven knew what the morrow would bring.

Emily regarded her brother with astonishment. "Lord Westwick is settling ten thousand pounds on Nell? But why?"

"Because he feels responsible for her situation, he says. And he minced no words about his opinion of my godmother's father for his refusal to provide for his granddaughter." Hugh smiled reminiscently. "Laid it all out on the table with no embroidery. You'd have loved hearing him, my dear."

"I certainly would! He is the most remarkable man, Hugh. For you won't credit what I've learned from Holmsly, either."

Hugh had disposed himself comfortably in his sister's drawing room, and watched now as she paced agitatedly around the room. "You know I've been upset that John leaves us alone so often with no explanation," she finally said, scowling at one of her son's toys before setting it aside. "He's gone for days at a time, saying only that he is off to Bristol."

"But he doesn't go to Bristol," Hugh suggested.

"You know that? Why didn't you tell me?"

"I don't know it for a fact. I have merely put two and two together, to come up with the possibility that John's mission is somewhere in the valley south of Bath."

Emily regarded him incredulously. "And you never said anything to me!"

"My dear sister, who am I to be casting doubt on my brother-in-law's word when I have no proof that I am correct? Twice I have heard of his being where he should not have been, and both those times he was south of Bath. That may be suspicious, but hardly a condemnation of him."

"Oh, Hugh, you will not credit it, but John has been working for Lord Westwick, managing his stud farm. You know what a genius John is with horses, and apparently we are quite poor! Well, not precisely poor, but not nearly so well off as I had believed. And he thought me incapable of the least economy. Truly! As though I could not be trusted to curtail my expenditures or exist quite cheerfully on half my allowance."

Hugh frowned as she came to a halt in front of him. "John would do better to start a stud of his own. Would that I could assist him in funding such an undertaking."

"But that is precisely what Lord Westwick is doing. They have an arrangement where John can claim every third horse that he trains for his own. In a year, he says, he will have the proper stock to make Walter's future secure." She smiled a little mistily. "I'm so proud of him, Hugh. And so grateful to Lord Westwick."

"The earl has been a busy man," Hugh murmured, and he proceeded to explain to her just what the earl had proposed to Miss Longstreet the previous evening.

"My word! The poor man cannot think marriage to Miss Longstreet would be anything but torture. How could he even suggest it?"

"He is attempting to make matters as right as he is able at this late date. I doubt she'll have him, though. Why should she, when all is said and done? She didn't love him, and though she could attempt to make his life miserable, I think it most unlikely she would succeed."

"But he adored his wife. I should think just being with someone else would be a most unhappy situation."

"Perhaps."

Emily perched on the edge of the chair opposite him. "And what do you intend to do, Hugh?"

"About what?"

"About Nell."

"Miss Armstrong is well provided for, Emily. She can have her choice of gentlemen in Bath or Westmorland."

"You cannot be so absurd. Don't forget that I know you, Hugh. I have watched you with Nell these last weeks, and I am aware that you have formed a *tendre* for her. Are you not going to offer for her?"

Hugh grimaced. "Unfortunately, I have waited a little too long to do that. If I were to offer for her now, she would have every reason to believe it was because of her new prosperity. And my godmother would label me a fortune hunter, you may be sure."

"So you would let your pride prevent you from offering for the woman you love?" asked Emily scornfully. "At least Lord Westwick let his heart speak for him when he was faced with a difficult choice! You don't deserve Nell if you would let such a paltry excuse stand in your way."

"Emily, I am thinking of Nell as well. She can make a much better match than I am at present. Trust me, she will be grateful."

"Oh, trust you, indeed! If she has, as I suspect, fallen in love with you, she will be brokenhearted!"

They were interrupted by the nursery maid bringing Walter for a visit, and no more was said on the subject. But Emily's eyes flashed when he left her with her son some time later, and he wondered if she could possibly be right.

Chapter Eighteen

Nell found that her aunt's mood had not improved significantly the next morning when they met at the breakfast table. The older woman stared balefully at her companion and demanded, "What did you say to Westwick to induce him to settle a fortune on you?"

"Now, Aunt, you know I would never discuss such a thing with Lord Westwick."

"But you've been spending time with him, haven't you, behind my back?"

"I believe I told you that without an explanation as to why I should repudiate him, I would not hold myself to obey your command on the subject."

Rosemarie snorted. "And had you known that he had broken his promise to me, would you then have been willing to cut him?"

Nell considered for a moment. "Well, it has always been clear to me that he is, in general, a kind and generous man, Aunt. I would have been hard-pressed to change that opinion, for one act, however reprehensible, in the distant past."

"No loyalty, that's your problem. His one reprehensible act was against me, your own aunt. That should weigh most heavily with you."

Nell nodded. "Perhaps it would have, had you explained. But you chose not to."

"I value my privacy."

"You certainly didn't seem to value your privacy at the Assembly Rooms last night."

Her aunt grunted. "Last night was my revenge on Westwick."

"It will certainly make his position in Bath difficult."

"As it should be. He has never had to suffer for his behavior."

"Oh, I doubt that, Aunt Longstreet. I imagine Lord Westwick has suffered a great deal for his decision. He's that kind of man, one who could not break an important societal rule without suffering the consequences. But he would do so quietly, not allowing his pain to be inflicted on others."

"Bah! You make him sound like a saint, Helen. Let me assure you he is not. He placed me in a distressing position, and my father only made matters more difficult."

"I understand that. What I'm saying is that Lord Westwick has perhaps tried to be a better person because of his mistakes as a young man."

"You only think that because he is settling a great deal of money on you."

Nell laughed. "You may be right. Aunt, are you aware that grandfather, when he was dying, made me promise to stay with you always?"

Her aunt set down knife and fork and stared at her niece. "Are you telling me that the only reason you've stayed with me is because of a promise to my father?"

"Of course not. I'm asking you if you knew of that promise. I would very much like to have an answer to my question."

Rosemarie regained her knife and fork and asked, "Why?"

"It's important to me."

"Hmmm. He may have said something of the sort, that you would stay with me. But it never occurred to me that you would go anywhere else."

"You didn't expect me to marry?"

"Of course not. How were you to meet anyone, and without a dowry, who would ally themselves with you?"

Nell sighed. "But, Aunt, don't you see how unfair that was to me?"

"Nonsense. You were being given a home and a family."

Nell decided no further attempt at bringing her aunt to an understanding was worth the effort. "Tell me, Aunt. Do you consider me to be bound by my promise to your father?"

"Why wouldn't you be?" her aunt demanded, eyes narrowed.

"Yes, I have always considered myself bound," Nell said thoughtfully. "Though I must admit that I did not make the promise entirely freely. I made it because your father was dying and demanded it of me. I did it to ease his mind, and because he had taken me in, even though I believe it was you who had truly accomplished that feat."

"My father, myself, what difference did it make? A bit self-serving to quibble about it at this late date."

"So, you expect me to spend the rest of your life with you, even if you decide to marry Lord Westwick?"

"Whether or not I marry Westwick has nothing to do with you."

"Does it not? You picture the three of us living together at Longstreet Manor?"

"I don't picture anything, missy. You made a promise, and you must abide by it."

"I see."

Nell continued eating her breakfast, her mind awhirl with thoughts, arguments, and speculations. But she was determined to know her own mind before she brought any of these ideas out into the light of day. Perhaps, after all, they would not be tested.

The afternoon had turned blustery by the time Nell made her way across Queen Square toward Milsom Street. In her basket she carried two library books and a swatch of fabric her aunt wanted thread to match. No one except Emily had come to call the whole day, which both surprised and disappointed Nell. Emily herself had been bursting with the news of her husband's secret mission, and if she knew of the various other developments in Nell's life, she did not let on. The two had chatted comfortably about all manner of things, but Sir Hugh's name had not come up. Emily had, however, renewed her offer to have Nell come to live with them, and Nell had, as before, thanked her and said that it was impossible.

As she hurried along now, the wind tugging at her skirts, she thought of stopping to order another dress from Madame de Vigne but could not quite bring herself to do so. Though so much had happened in the last twenty-four hours, there was little evidence of change. Was her life to go on much as before, except that she would have a bigger allowance? Was she bound to Aunt Longstreet until the older woman died? And would that really matter?

Sir Hugh saw Nell just as she was about to enter the circulating library. When he signaled that he wished her to wait for him, she looked as though she might slip into the building instead. As he came up to her, he exclaimed, "I was on my way to Queen Square, Nell! I would have a word with you in private if I might."

"I have a few errands to accomplish, if you wish to accompany me," she suggested, lowering her gaze. "The library first."

"Of course."

He followed her into the building and up the stairs to the very place where he had first seen her, caught between his overbearing godmother and the long-suffering librarian. He had tried to deflect attention onto himself, thinking the poor young woman would be incapable of handling the situation.

But he had found Nell more than capable of standing up to her aunt. The librarian smiled at her now, calling them both by name, and offering any service of which he might be capable. Nell assured him she had nothing more than a pair of books to return.

"I have put aside for you another novel by the lady who wrote *Mansfield Park*," he whispered when Nell leaned forward to hand him the books. "I knew you would be pleased."

"Oh, thank you, Mr. Bentley. How kind." Nell smiled conspiratorially and slipped the volumes into her basket. "I shall be certain to return them as soon as I am finished."

"Take your time, take your time," he begged her. "With so much as there is to do in Bath, I know one's reading time is limited."

Hugh was not surprised by the admiring gleam in the librarian's eyes. He could only hope it had no more influence on Nell than the brisk breeze that met them on their descent back into Milsom Street. "More errands?" he asked, a quizzical tone to his voice.

"Just one more. I wish to match some thread for my aunt."

"Stokers, then," he suggested and placed her hand on his arm. She looked up at him with such a sweet, tentative expression on her face that he ached to kiss her right there in the street. Instead, he said gruffly, "I take it Miss Longstreet is not unduly impressed by your change in circumstances."

"Oh, no. She expects we will go on much as we have, I believe."

Hugh's brow drew down. "And what do you expect?"

"I hardly know. Aunt Longstreet will not even tell me what she plans to do about Lord Westwick's offer."

"Do you think she'll have him?"

"No. I think she will prefer to go on as we have."

Hugh was thunderstruck. "But, Nell, you cannot mean you will stay with her."

His companion sighed. "I believe I told you about my promise to my grandfather."

"She means to hold you to it, does she?"

Nell nodded, but she had turned her head away so that Hugh could not see her eyes. "And you intend to make the best of that, as you have of everything else in your life?" he demanded.

"Did you hear Emily's news, about her husband?"

"Don't try to change the subject, Nell. This is important. Miss Longstreet can't hold you to a promise you made to her father on his deathbed."

"I doubt there is a more sacred promise than one made to a dying person," she returned. "It is surely as compelling as a promise of marriage, such as Lord Westwick made to her."

"And, in this case, just as despicably held to." His eyes flashed. "You read her letters, Nell. The earl attempted to get her to free him of his promise, and she would not do it, though it must have been perfectly obvious to her—and perhaps to her family—that he had changed his mind."

"Yes." Nell regarded him steadily for a moment. "Sir Hugh, you mustn't fret on my behalf. I shall be perfectly content to stay at Longstreet Manor."

"Nonsense! You . . . you should be thinking of marriage."

"Should I?" She paused on the pavement before Stokers and smiled pertly at him. "And who should I be thinking of marrying?"

"Me!" What a muff he was making of this, declaring himself in the middle of the street in Bath. But her face softened, and she sighed. "Thank you. I would that it were possible."

"Well, it is possible," he insisted. "I know I should have spoken before, Nell, but I wanted to see this matter of my godmother and Lord Westwick cleared up first, and now everything has crashed in at once. You mustn't think that the change in your circumstances has anything to do with my offer, for it hasn't."

"Of course not," she agreed, readily enough. "But there is no change in one very important aspect of my circumstances. So, we will speak no more of the matter."

With this, she pushed open the door of Stokers' store and entered. A very annoying bell tinkled raucously for some moments as Hugh tried to gather his thoughts together. She had turned him down. Was her promise merely an excuse?

Nell headed directly to the display of threads, pulling a swatch of fabric from her basket. Hugh hadn't realized how many variations of color there would be, with spools lined up in two drawers. Nell bent to consider a section where blue and green threads proliferated. Hugh came to stand behind her.

"If Miss Longstreet were to free you from your promise . . ." he began.

"She won't." Nell placed the swatch of cloth beside one of the spools, but the thread was too dark.

"Nell, it isn't fair of her to hold you to it."

"No. Aunt Longstreet is not always fair."

"Then, you will have to break your promise."

She regarded him with solemn eyes. "I can't do that, Hugh."

"But you must!"

She smiled sadly but did not answer. Picking up another spool of thread, she compared it to her fabric, and set it down again.

"Your grandfather did not envision the change in your circumstances. He didn't even know for certain of your . . . well, you understand," he said, glancing around the shop to see if anyone was within earshot. There was no one else in the shop at all except the shopkeeper, who was busy refolding some untidy bolts of cloth at the far end of the room. "Nell, he would have wished you to have a life of your own."

"No, he wouldn't. He was just as self-absorbed and un-caring as Aunt Longstreet."

Hugh grimaced. "Yes, I remember. Well, then he had no business extracting such a promise from you."

"Perhaps not, but he did. I can't change that, Hugh." She picked up another spool of thread, matched it, and said, "This one will do."

When she had paid for her purchase and dropped it into her basket, they turned their footsteps in the direction of Queen Square. Hugh tried once again. "Nell, no one would hold it against you if you broke such a disagreeable and un-fair promise. In fact, no one would even know."

"You would know, and I would know, and Aunt Longstreet would know. Even Emily would know. You're the most important people in my life, and you would all know that I hadn't kept a promise merely because it was in-convenient for me."

"Inconvenient! Heaven help us, it is a great deal more than inconvenient. And, Nell, you have seen what Lord Westwick did in the same circumstances. His own happiness was more important to him than his honor."

"No, the happiness of his beloved was more important to him, Hugh. If it had been merely his own happiness, I do not think he would have broken his promise."

"And isn't my happiness important to you?" he asked, his voice low and intense.

"I . . . I don't think . . . It's not the same."

"Isn't it? You don't truly believe in my love for you, do you, Nell?"

"I . . . Of course I do. It is just . . ."

"Then, it is your own love for me which you don't trust."

"No!" Nell's cheeks flushed hotly. "We're not like Lord Westwick and his lady. We're not the stuff of legends. At least, I am not, Hugh! You must see that. I'm just an ordi-nary girl, someone who has been companion to her aunt for years and is given to daydreaming and flights of fancy. I feel as though I've made you up, invented you. Nothing like this could really happen to a simple country lady like myself. I will leave Bath, and you will go on with your life as though I had never been."

"Impossible." He brushed a thumb along the line of her jaw, bemused. "You didn't make me up, my love, you merely made me fall in love with you. How could I not have? All your strength and good humor in the face of adversity. All your enthusiasm and excitement about the simplest treats. You are the most remarkable woman I've ever met—practical and whimsical, generous and competent. I love you dearly, Nell."

"Oh, Hugh." She turned her face up to him, her lips trembling, and suddenly he was kissing her—right there in front of the Queen Square house! Her body leaned toward him, as though he were the sun and source of her very survival.

"Will you marry me?"

"Oh, Hugh, you know I cannot!"

"Will you marry me if you do not have to break your promise?"

Her eyes blinked in confusion. "Oh, Hugh, I love you. Of course I would marry you if I didn't have to break my promise."

He smiled ruefully. "Very well. She can't live forever, the wicked woman. I daresay we can avoid her now and again. Longstreet Manor is a large house."

"But . . . You cannot mean to . . ."

"Yes, my adorable Nell. If living at the Manor is the only way I can have you as my bride, then live there I shall. She does intend to leave it to me, you know. I might as well reacquaint myself with the place."

"But . . . but what if she should accept Lord Westwick?"

"The place will be a little crowded, to be sure, but we'll manage. And I cannot think she would object to your accompanying me to Fallings from time to time, then. In fact, I shall insist upon it, even if she doesn't marry the earl."

Nell burst into tears. Hugh had never seen her cry before, and only realized after a few moments of dabbing at the moisture with his handkerchief that they were tears of happiness. "Come, my sweet. There is nothing to cry about. We'll tell Emily first. She's been planning to make you her sister-in-law, and will be delighted to hear that she has once again been successful in one of her schemes."

Rosemarie was nonplussed. She looked from Nell to Sir Hugh and said bluntly, "He can't live at Longstreet Manor."

"Of course he can," Nell retorted. "There's plenty of room, and if I'm going to marry him, he'll *have* to live there."

"You aren't going to marry him. You promised to stay with me as long as I live."

"And so I shall, Aunt. I didn't promise not to marry; I promised only to stay with you, and I intend to do precisely that. Sir Hugh is your heir, and it makes sense that he should spend time at Longstreet Manor, in any case."

"I can change my will," her aunt stated flatly. "I can leave my estate to someone else."

"Yes, but you have *promised*, have you not?" Nell asked innocently. "As I have. I think—in fact I am quite certain—that if you decided not to honor your promise to Sir Hugh, I would feel released from my promise to my grandfather."

"I think she has you there, ma'am," Sir Hugh said with a grin. "Your niece is a very honorable young woman, but she expects her conviction to be met with a similar commitment."

"You can't tell me you won't be haring off to Fallings all the time," his godmother suggested slyly. "*Then* what will missy do? Take off with you, or I miss my bet."

"Sometimes she will, sometimes she won't," Sir Hugh

said. "She isn't indentured to you, Miss Longstreet. He
promise to stay with you does not—to my mind, at least—
trap her at Longstreet Manor for every day of her life. Ne
will reside there, but make trips whenever she pleases—t
Fallings, to Bath, to London—just as any young lad
might."

"He's marrying you for your money!" Rosemarie snappe
to her niece.

But Nell only laughed. "Poor fellow. Some men woul
not think there was enough money in the entire world to off
set having to live away from their own homes."

And she realized as she said it that it was what Lord West
wick had done, as well. For the love of his life, he had give
up his family estate and established himself in Bath with hi
countess. Not quite the same as living with a cantankerou
lady like Aunt Longstreet, but just as much proof of his love
Nell twined her arm with Sir Hugh's and asked gently
"Won't you wish us happy, Aunt Longstreet?"

"If I decide to accept Westwick, I won't have you two liv
ing at Longstreet Manor and underfoot all the time. Is tha
clear?"

"Yes, ma'am," they both said together.

"But you can visit, now and again. That would be al
right."

"Yes, ma'am."

"That's *if* I accept him."

Nell and Sir Hugh said nothing.

"It's not a sure thing that I will."

"No, ma'am." But we can hope, Nell thought, and Si
Hugh squeezed her arm.

"And don't go trying to influence me."

"No, ma'am."

Rosemarie's gaze dropped slightly before Nell's determined look. "And I do wish you happy," she said grudgingly.

"Thank you."

There was a knock at the front door. Nell knew it would be Lord Westwick, come for his reluctant bride's decision. She watched as her aunt, most uncharacteristically, patted her hair into place and tossed the shawl off her knees. "Run along, now, you two. I've seen enough of this April and May. I want a word in private with Westwick."

Nell, her eyes sparkling, led her intended from the room. When the earl had greeted them and moved on to face his dragon in the parlor, Nell urged Hugh down the hall to the study. "She's going to accept him!" she whispered as he closed the door behind them.

"Thank heaven!" he replied, pulling her into his arms and capturing her lips with his.